SHOOTING STAR

Martin Waddell is the winner of the prestigious 2004 Hans Christian Andersen Award – the international prize presented every two years to an author whose complete works have made an important and lasting contribution to children's literature. He has written many classic and award-winning picture books, and his novels for older readers have also received widespread acclaim, including *The Life and Loves of Zoë T. Curley*, *The Kidnapping of Suzie Q*, *Tango's Baby* and his trilogy about the Troubles in Northern Ireland: *Starry Night* (winner of the Other Award, runner-up for the Guardian Children's Fiction Prize and shortlisted for the Young Observer Teenage Fiction Prize), *Frankie's Story* and *The Beat of the Drum*. He lives with his wife, Rosaleen, in Newcastle, County Down, Northern Ireland.

Books by the same author

The Kidnapping of Suzie Q
The Life and Loves of Zoë T. Curley
Starry Night
Frankie's Story
The Beat of the Drum
Tango's Baby

SHOOTING STAR
MARTIN WADDELL

WALKER BOOKS
AND SUBSIDIARIES
LONDON • BOSTON • SYDNEY • AUCKLAND

This is a work of fiction. Names, characters, places and incidents are either the product of the author's imagination or, if real, are used fictitiously.

First published 2004 by Walker Books Ltd
87 Vauxhall Walk, London SE11 5HJ

2 4 6 8 10 9 7 5 3 1

Text © 2004 Martin Waddell
Cover photograph © Mike Powell/Getty Images

This book has been typeset in Sabon

Printed in Great Britain by Cox & Wyman Ltd, Reading, Berkshire

British Library Cataloguing in Publication Data:
a catalogue record for this book
is available from the British Library

ISBN 0-7445-6574-X

www.walkerbooks.co.uk

For John Joseph Harrison,

one for the Toon

TO KICK OFF WITH...

My name is Mickey Griff ... ex-footballer, two Welsh caps, fourteen years as a pro, four in the top flight with Everton and Leicester City ... a journeyman footballer at best. Since I quit playing I've made a living as a backroom boy in the Nationwide, Conference, Doc Martens, Rymans. I've tried my hand as manager, coach, scout, player's agent, sporting consultant, radio and TV chat merchant. You name it, I've done it ... wherever they would have me.

You may have heard of me, you may not, but that doesn't matter ... because this is Buzzer Jezz's story, not mine.

After his two goals against Spain in Madrid no one in the game would dispute that Buzz *is England's brightest young prospect in a generation.*

The dinks and jinks, the blistering pace, the hat-trick in his first full Premiership outing against Liverpool ... that's Buzzer Jezz. Giggs and Owen and Bellamy and Dyer and Joe Cole eat your hearts out. If Buzz keeps on the way he is headed, he'll finish out there in front of you, up with the Maradonas and the Pelés ... that's what I reckon. Maybe I'm biased in his favour, but still ... his goal-scoring record speaks for itself.

The tabloids have poured out thousands of words about young Buzz's personal life since the boy burst onto the Premiership scene ... but I'm not interested in that junk.

Buzz is a footballer. He made his name on the pitch, and it is what he did on the pitch in the early days before he made it in the Premiership and into England's World Cup squad that I'm qualified to write about.

That's what you'll find in this book – Buzz's story, told through the games that mattered ... the turning points in his early career.

I was there when it first started to happen for him, long before his breakthrough. I'm not trying to claim that I made Buzz or changed his game ... nobody made Buzzer Jezz ... he is unique, a one-off ... but I gave him the lift he needed, when he most needed it.

This is a footballer's story, told by a football fanatic, for other football fanatics. If that isn't your bag, switch off now.

TOWN v TOTTENHAM HOTSPUR

YOUTH MATCH
VENUE: GREELEY PARK

For me, Buzzer Jezz's story starts at Greeley Park, which is the ground Town used for youth games.

It was the first time I saw him play, and I'll never forget it – he made *that* big an impression.

I was youth development officer at Town when Teddy Maher was manager there – my only berth at a league club as it turned out – and we had Tottenham coming down to us.

This game is a big number for my lads.

Tottenham Hotspur are a very important lump of Cheddar indeed when compared to Town. Turn it on against Spurs and my lads might find themselves moving up.

OK, it doesn't often work that way, but it *can* – that's what you're hoping if you're a young player who believes he might just be the next Giggs or Owen or Beckham. They have to believe that, or they wouldn't be out there, would they?

We don't undeceive them. We *want* them believing. The believing really matters. Don't let anyone kid you with the line that *results don't matter at youth level*. Results do matter … to the lads. And in this case they mattered to me as well, because my work prospects were looking dodgy, to say the least.

So we have our lads built up for the game. We're at them all week, telling them, *This is your chance … go out and do it*. Come match day, they are one hundred per cent fired up, going to go out there and show all these Tottenham starlets that we are no easy touch.

This is the White Hart Lane bunch that included Steve Bower – yes, *that* Steve Bower – and Greencroft, who went to Man City, and Willie Grover, who is with Villa. They have Adam Croxley in goal and Ward Collins out wide on the right.

And Buzzer Jezz, a year and a bit younger than them, but right in there with the best.

So we have Spurs … at home, and my lads are keyed up to go at them right from the start – stretch them, close them down, let them know they are in a game. *Work at it. Show them you can play a bit.* I've given the lads all those lines, and now they are out there.

Only it doesn't work out as planned.

As soon as the game kicked off they were at us, big time ... all over us. My lads were chasing shadows.

Bower was bossing everything, tackling like a tank, cajoling, teasing, playing balls our lads couldn't read. You could see even then that he was going to be the great player he is. If anything, he looked even better then because he was an early developer, Bower. He had the legs and the build. Our little lads just bounced off him ... when they got close, which wasn't often. He was in midfield, working forward ... something quite different to his game now that Spurs have built their defence around him.

We're getting the runaround.

They are two up after fifteen minutes, and cruising.

My manager, Teddy Maher, has come down to run his eye over our talent ... and Teddy does not like what he sees. On the mini-budget I have at Town, when compared with the White Hart Lane set-up, he has no reason to complain. They ought to be able to beat us. If they didn't, there would be questions asked.

Still, Teddy is sitting there, looking glum, as though I've let him down somehow.

"You want to get someone on that big lad pronto, Mickey," he tells me, giving me the benefit of his deep insight into the game.

I know that of course. My lads have been trying, as instructed, but I haven't a player who can live with Steve Bower. What Teddy means is that as the officially labelled youth development officer at Town I *should* have someone who can do it.

Youth development officer ... that's a joke ... big title, but there was only me for the youth team work. I did everything, from laying out the shirts to making sure that the water was hot, plus whatever coaching I could fit in. Town hired me on a part-time basis: three nights a week, and Saturdays. The truth is they didn't have a youth development plan worthy of the name, because Teddy had no intention of still being there when the kids came of age.

"Some player, that lad," he tells me again.

And he sits there, admiring Bower and letting me see that he doesn't reckon my lads, any of them. That wasn't fair. I had two or three who might have made it and one who did. Leroy Elms went on to play four seasons with Notts County, and some of the others turned out in the lower leagues. For a team like Town, that's not bad going, considering we don't have the pick of the bunch to begin with, the way the glamour clubs do.

13

Face it, who is going to join Town if they have Manchester United or Arsenal or Chelsea asking? The only way round that problem is to go outside the rules and wave chequebooks at their dads. But a chequebook to wave is something that Teddy and Town haven't given me.

Well, I'm admiring Bower too. Bower you can't miss. He is dominating the game, but there is another little kid out there on the pitch who keeps catching my eye. He is in and out of it a bit, but when he *is* in he really shows.

It's Buzz, but I don't know that then.

Because Buzz hasn't become *Buzz* yet, if you see what I mean.

He's small and Tottenham are playing him out wide on the left. I have Tom Sturges against him. Tom went to Bath City and played all right. Later he moved to Dorking, before he did his knee. Tom's big and he's quick. I have him marking up tight, and he's knocking the little lad about, the way you do when you're facing a shrimp with fast feet.

The little lad keeps coming back at him for more, and he is giving Tom a tough time – a very tough time – picking himself up after Tom's kicked him. Basically he is taking Tom to the cleaners, and Tom is a kid I rely on at the back.

As Town's coach I don't like what is happening to Tom, but as a football nut I have to take time out and admire what the little kid is doing to him.

I also like the runs young Buzz is making every time he gets off Tom. I'm yelling at my lads to give Tom cover, because something could go wrong if he's left exposed by the kid's pace.

That's just what happened.

Bower is on the ball, wide left, just inside Spurs' half. He looks like he's heading in field, then suddenly he flicks the ball behind Tom, and the little kid is *there*, ghosting out of nowhere. His speed has him steaming clear down the touchline, goal-side of Tom, with the big defender on his heels, and my cover coming across. He does a shuffle, still going full pace, and he's past the cover, six yards from the goal-line.

Now he's cutting into the box at a narrow angle.

Tom has done wonders to get back, and he lunges in. Buzz senses the tackle coming, skips over Tom's leg ... but Tom's done enough in my book – taken him off balance and driven him close to the goal line, so there is almost no angle left for a shot.

Feet is a Buzz-thing I didn't know about then.

Somehow he keeps his balance, hurdling

Tom's heavy challenge, stumbling, but, incredibly, keeping control of the ball. He's in full flight, and the ball's still glued to him ... though he's only got a yard or so to work in before he runs out of pitch.

The keeper has come tight on his near post to narrow what's left of the angle ... which is almost nothing. In theory, he's left the net open to a delicate lob to the far post ... but bringing off a lob like that needs the kind of pinpoint accuracy the keeper is entitled not to expect.

That's how the keeper reads it anyway. Buzzer reads it that way too, but goes for it just the same. Half falling as he hits the ball, he chips the keeper and goes sprawling onto the running track. The ball floats across the face of the goal, strikes the angle of the bar and the far post and gets cleared.

Buzz should have gone down when Tom lunged at him – odds-on, a penalty would have been given. The boy could have cut the ball back – but there was only one Spurs player coming in, Collins, and I have two defenders on cover. Or he could have turned away from goal, shepherding the ball, and laying it out wide for the support player.

Three options, then, that any player in the pro game would recognize.

But Buzz isn't just any player. He's got his mind set on scoring after the way he's burst clear of the defence. Taking on the chip took nerve and a whole cupboardful of self-belief.

"You were lucky that time, Mickey," Teddy says, glowering at me. "Little kid should have cut it back, or gone down, looking for the penalty."

"He nearly scored," I say, carefully, remembering I'm hanging on by my fingernails to this job, and it's a job I need, so I have to keep Teddy on side and in my camp.

I should have let it pass. Nothing I could say was going to make Teddy appreciate what he'd just seen, was it?

"I'd have him for that if I was in Ray Clinton's shoes," Teddy responds.

That's why Teddy's teams get the results they get, round the bottom of Division Two or Three.

The game goes on, and I'm liking it – not as Town's youth coach, because we're being run ragged, but because I'm seeing things happen the way they ought to, if you have kids who can play and a youth coach like Ray Clinton, who lets them do it their own way. Give them the basics, OK, in small doses, but don't kill the other stuff in their heads that makes them special.

Ray's kids are playing the game the way it should be. Running and grafting and finding each other with little one-twos and lay-offs and triangles. Lovely to watch, if it isn't your team they're putting through the mangle. But you can't help enjoying it, can you? The part of you that cares about the game loves that stuff, while the part of you that has to sort out some kind of rescue plan for coping with it at half-time is going wild in the head.

Bower again, halfway line, nowhere to go. He's just won the ball, and Buzz is back behind him, covering, out of position ... so no ball to Buzz is on.

Bower moves inside, drawing Tom on, and Buzz cuts across his back, on a diagonal run.

And it is *beautiful*.

Bower steps over the ball and leaves it behind him.

Buzz is onto it and away in a flash, hugging the touchline, with Tom nowhere, still following Bower's run that never was.

So Buzz is clear wide, and Bower has left poor Tom floundering and is powering straight down the middle, howling for the ball back. My central defender has to choose between Bower and Buzz, and he goes for the man on the ball.

Buzz stops dead as the defender comes at him.

Then he jinks, then he dinks, and he has the defender going. Release it, and Bower is clear in on goal. Buzz does go to release it, but he jinks again first, and it is a jink too far – he's still prone to overdoing that one –

he miscontrols the ball and it rolls into touch.

Buzz thumbs up Bower for the step-over, grinning. His too-big shirt is out, flopping round his little spindly legs – like Pinocchio in football boots. Bower stands there with his hands on his hips, looking disgusted.

"Reminds me of Johnny Haynes and Tosh Chamberlain down at Fulham, way back," Teddy says, reminiscing again. "Tosh played outside Johnny ... the old left-wing position. Ran like a hare ... shot like a rocket ... only they were unguided missiles. Used to break poor Johnny's heart. Robbo's too. Haynes and Robson and the young Mullery ... some combination ... but what they had to pass to was Tosh!"

Me, I *don't* remember Tosh Chamberlain. Never heard of him. I wasn't even born when Haynes and Bobby Robson played for England. I've seen Alan Mullery commentating on TV. Come to think of it, Mullery said some nice words about me on Sky once ... they tell me he did anyway. What Teddy Maher is doing is telling me about his wealth of experience in the game. My playing career was in the eighties, early nineties. As far as Teddy is concerned, I'm still wet behind the ears. Teddy, no doubt, taught Robbo all he knows about management, and put Johnny Haynes right on a few things as well.

19

"Didn't know you was at Fulham in their glory days back in the sixties, Ted," I said, sounding innocent.

Teddy was a Northampton/Grimsby Town/Chesterfield-class, low-grade tank of a mid-fielder when he played, despite the big name he made for himself later as a Sky TV guru. I just couldn't resist letting him know it. At least I'd *played* at the top in the old First Division, and briefly in the Premiership too, after the change-over. Luckily, Teddy wasn't listening to what I was saying. He never did. That's how highly he rated me as a coach.

The game goes on.

We're coming back into it, playing some nice stuff, but nothing is going our way. Round about the fortieth minute Collins gets one of his trademark goals, cutting inside and slotting it to the near post, when the keeper had read it the other way.

Town 0 – Tottenham Hotspur 3, half-time.

"Better sort your lads out in the dressing room," Teddy tells me aggressively, and he goes off to natter with his mates about the big-timer he used to be.

That leaves me with my lads to cope with … and there's not a lot I can say, is there? I reorganize a bit, move my wideman back to double-mark Buzz with Tom, and try telling them all to keep the ball out of Bower's areas. What else can I do? They've played hard.

They've run themselves off their feet. And we are three goals down and we won't get them back.

That's *not* what I tell them, but they know it, and heads are down despite all I'm saying about it being a game of two halves, and how they should go out and do it.

As it happens, we didn't do too badly in the second half.

I have two against one on Buzzer's side. He should have coped with the extra man – Buzz would *now*, no question – but the little bit of special attention Tom was giving him kept the boy under control … more or less.

Buzz wasn't the finished article then. What's here is a baby footballer, who still has a lot of growing to do. Not many players in their early teens can do it non-stop right through a game, certainly not one who's knee-high to a grasshopper, like Buzz. That's hard fact. The body strength just isn't there.

Buzz was the youngest kid on the field, giving most of the others a long start. The way the Spurs coach reckoned it, we were easy meat, and he's brought Buzz in to see how he gets on with the big lads.

Well, Buzz has showed him … and he's still trying to show him, but Tom's coping better in this half. Tom's strong. He's bustling Buzz, jockeying … driving him onto the extra man I'd added in his areas, or forcing him wide.

And Buzz just hadn't the legs or the know-how to pull off him.

So we had two men marking one most of the time, leaving us a man short going forward.

Bower is still running things.

He reads what has happened to Buzz and now he switches his game and he's playing long balls to Collins.

Collins is doing what Buzz had been doing – differently, because their styles are different, but equally effectively.

Lovely to watch, but we lose two more goals. It's 0–5.

The fifth one is a peach.

It is Buzz, coming briefly back on song just when it seemed he'd faded out of the game. He does what has since become his trademark.

He gets the ball midfield, where he's wandered inside, trying to lose Tom.

This time he pulls off a little back-heeler in mid-stride, switches direction back the way he was heading before, and leaves Tom floundering.

The kid I have doubling up the marking with Tom comes crashing in ... bad tackle, studs up. Doesn't matter ... Buzz jumps the tackle, and he's away with the ball at his feet.

Twenty yards out, still going, defenders closing in... Nothing for us to panic about, because he has no support, has he?

Didn't need it.

The shot is hit like a rocket, drilled so hard that it was a goal almost before it left his boot. Any keeper playing in the Premiership these days will tell you that – when Buzz hits one right, no one stops it.

The ball crashes past the keeper, swerving just inside the left upright.

You've seen him do it. Everybody has ... now. Not then. There's nothing to suggest he's going to hit it ... he just does it, somehow. No back-lift. Nothing.

Keeper doesn't even move.

The net balloons from the sheer force of the strike. Power like Hasslebank, or Roberto Carlos.

I'll say it again ... no back-lift that I could see. There was nothing to let the keeper guess what was coming.

Buzz takes off. He's got his arms in the air; then it's handsprings and a somersault.

"Knows how to milk it, doesn't he?" Teddy Maher says sourly. "Don't like to see that in a young player."

He's fidgeting and looking at his gold watch, and I'm sitting there in awe at what I have just seen.

How did a kid with such a little body bring off a rocket like that?

Where does the power come from?

You tell me. I suppose it's just *Buzz*... That's what everyone knows him for now. Nothing complicated about it, if you can do it ... but only one player in a million can.

So what's Teddy the expert's line, as he departs in disgust well before the final whistle?

"Could have gone anywhere!" he tells me. "Hit and hope! I blame the keeper. See you in the office."

That's it really. Though I don't read the *see you in the office* right.

I'm too busy in my football head to realize that Teddy's not only seen enough of my team ... he's seen enough of his youth development officer as well.

Three days later, I was out of a job, doing the lower league rounds to find myself a fill-in that would see me through financially to the end of the season.

But *that* day, as Teddy stalked off, I was only thinking about Buzz, and the great player he's going to be if he keeps what he's got and can learn the rest. Love to have him in my team, I would. But you don't get young players like Buzz at a set-up like I've got. Take one look at our broken-down facilities at Town, they would, and they'd be off somewhere else, where the grass is greener.

Ten minutes more of that half, and Ray brings Buzz off.

Owen Temple goes on. Good kid. Built like a giraffe. He went on to play two years in and out of the first team at Spurs, then had a good run at Coventry City, where he won an England under-21 cap.

The point is that Temple is playing at his right age-level that day. He has a good measure of talent and potential, and still Ray has put the much younger Buzz on in front of him.

That's how highly Ray and Tottenham rated Buzzer Jezz *then*...

But soon after that, his football career went pear-shaped.

DOG AND DUCK v DUCK AND DOG

DOG AND DUCK LEAGUE

VENUE: PITCH 15, PRISON END, WORMWOOD
SCRUBS, WEST LONDON

Buzz had been on schoolboy terms at White Hart Lane from the day he first kicked his rattle out of the pram. But as with so many young players, early promise seemed to have come to nothing.

That's the way it goes. It happens to hundreds of kids who make a bright start, and then are never heard of again.

In Buzz's case, bad luck, injuries and a serious illness interrupted his progress. While the pick of the other kids in his White Hart Lane bunch moved on to greater things, Buzz fell far behind. Soon he lost all confidence in his own ability to perform at the top level.

He was going nowhere in footballing terms, and that about sums it up.

That's what Spurs thought, anyway.

They released him.

It was Ray Clinton's biggest mistake in his long life in the game. Ray said it himself on Sky, after Buzz turned it on against Man U this season. Two away goals at Old Trafford! No one on the TV panel disagreed with him. No one could, after the runaround Buzz had given the Man U defenders.

Ray's mistake meant that a bitterly disappointed Buzz walked away from the White Hart Lane set-up, his boots wrapped in a Marks & Spencer's bag, vowing to give up the game for ever.

So why did it hit Buzz so hard that he decided to quit, instead of trying to get fixed up somewhere else?

I reckon it this way. Tottenham was Buzz's team and Ray Clinton was the man who'd been building him. In Buzz's book, his youth coach was a football god and could do no wrong. Kids often see it that way. So when Spurs showed him the exit, Buzz accepted the verdict and, head bowed, turned his back on the game, and travelled home to Shepherd's Bush to break the sad news to his mum and dad.

Great journey home that must have been – Buzz with his boots in a bag and no future at Spurs.

The Buzzer Jezz story could have ended there. But it didn't...

The second time I saw Buzz play was a long time later, in a Sunday morning Dog and Duck kick-about game at Wormwood Scrubs in West London. I'm glad I went down Du Cane Road that morning. What I saw there changed my life – and his!

That Sunday, the Sunday I went dog walking on Wormwood Scrubs, my involvement in the game had changed a bit from my so-called glory days at Town under Teddy Maher.

I'd just taken on managing part-time at Hollins and Parborough, normally a bottom-half-of-the-Conference team. I'd come to Boro after an eighteen-month stint coaching at Dagenham and Redbridge, a spell in charge at St Albans, then a few weeks with Weymouth – about which the less said the better. I'd filled in the gaps with some journo hack work, combined with scouting for Orient and Millwall, and later Bournemouth, but on a piecework basis, little more than beer money.

Buzz ... well, when I see him I don't even know it's Buzz I'm looking at. I'm just wandering round the pitches at the prison end, looking at the play the way you do ... always hoping you'll see something special there.

You seldom, if ever, do. I'm thinking about yesterday's pre-season friendly, when St Albans City did us down at their place, and wondering what I can do to get some life back into Boro.

The game is in one of the West London Dog and Duck leagues. There must be twenty or thirty games going on that morning, with the pitches back-to-back.

And I see this little kid playing at the back. He hasn't the height for it … but he's got the *sense* of it, the way very few park players do. He's not bothering much, but everything that comes near him he's picking out, and when he has got it he's spraying the ball around.

He's in what looks like a pub team. They are big lads, full-grown men, but not real players. This kid is the exception. He's under age – I doubt if a pub could legally serve him. More interestingly, he's dominating everything. All he is doing is reading the angles and laying the ball off when he's got it, but the balls he's laying off aren't wasted.

And I think, *I've seen him before somewhere*, only I don't connect him with Tottenham, two or three years before, when he was a wideman with little stick-insect legs. Why would I? There's so many of them – so many kids you see, and you think, *Yes, maybe, if…* And then you never hear of them again.

The Scrubs is not where you expect to see Academy-level starlets, is it?

The team he's with is no Tottenham either. The goalie must weigh eighteen stone, and they only have ten men, because someone didn't turn up. The striker plays like my old granny. There's nothing professional about this outfit.

Except for this kid. What I'm seeing stops me in my tracks.

All this huffing and puffing and rushing about is going on, hack merchants are hacking, the ball is a balloon, the ref is whistle-mad ... and in the middle of it is this lad, playing some lovely, lovely, lovely stuff. He has a kind of nonchalance on the ball that sticks out a mile in the kick-and-rush mayhem going on around him.

He's sturdy and well-built, but not tall enough for the job he's doing. He's out of position – in so far as they have positions. Presumably he's playing at the back for the fun of it. He's laughing and joking, just mucking about.

But ... when he tackles, he wins the ball.

When they play the ball in low, he's on it.

When they play the ball in high, he's read it, and he's up above these pub-team six-footers like a bird.

When he has the ball, he walks round them. He's skipping tackles, making little runs, laying it off before he needs to. He's working at half-speed, but that's all he needs. They are running around killing themselves, and he's not even in second gear.

Just once, he decides to take them on by himself. There's a gap on the left and he makes for it.

The ball finds him.

Thirty or forty yards from goal.

They're closing in on him ... three of them. Jink, dink, inside, out ... and he's away.

Just that one burst of pace, ten ... fifteen yards and the goalie starts off his line because the kid is clean through.

The kid looks up, suddenly slows his run, steadies himself... He's got all the time in the world, because he's left the defenders way behind him with his sudden burst.

Sees the goalie on the penalty spot. He's still ten ... fifteen yards outside the area.

One minute the ball is at his feet and the next he juggles it up ... and he volleys it, soft touch lob.

The ball dips under the bar ... goal.

Not what you see on a park pitch – a goal like that. Not one of Buzz's trademark rockets either. Just an exercise in perfection and precision – the perfect eye to see it and the precise skill to execute it.

The kid takes off. Arms in the air, hand-springs and the somersault.

Something clicks in my mind. *It's him. From years ago. He was in Spurs' dream bunch: Steve Bower, Ward Collins, Adam Croxley.* They're already on the edge of the Spurs first-team squad. Apart from Croxley, that is, who's on loan in goal at Stoke City, and getting his name in the papers after a run of six clean sheets in row – which doesn't happen that often at Stoke.

What has happened to this kid from the same bunch, who had as much potential as any of them? Of course, he was the baby of the Tottenham lot he played with. He'd not have had time yet to reach full body strength. But what's he doing larking about and playing Dog and Duck at the Scrubs, which is a far cry from White Hart Lane?

I wait and I go on the pitch after the whistle goes.

"You had a good game, son," I tell him.

"You reckon so?" he says, not taking much notice.

"I've seen you before," I tell him. "I've seen you better places. What are you doing slumming it?"

He doesn't say anything, but the grin goes.

"Matt Jezz," I say, remembering his name at last. You get a kind of file in your brain for players you fancy. It was years since I'd seen him play, and then just the once in a kids' game. Never heard tell of him since. But the name still stayed in my head. That's how much the baby-Buzz had impressed me. "They called you Buzzer, because you were always buzzing about."

He nods, reluctantly. The defences are up.

"You were on Tottenham's books," I tell him. "Right?"

"Yeah," he says curtly, turning his head away. "Used to be."

"What do you mean, *used to be*?" I say. He's still a kid ... how could it be *used to be*?

"I don't play the game for real no more," he says uneasily. "I quit."

"You quit Spurs' youth outfit ... for this?"

"I'm not with Spurs no more, am I?" he says. "And this isn't *playing*. This is just messing about with a few mates."

There was an uncomfortable and almost cocky defiance in the way he said it, but there was a tinge of anger as well.

"OK," I say. "OK, son. Calm down. Sorry I spoke. Just, I'm in the game, and I saw you play before. Liked what I saw," I add, softening it a bit.

He didn't take it well.

"I was out injured," he says. "Right? And they gave me the treatment. I'm fine now. But I'd lost my place in the queue and Spurs dumped me. I'm out. End of story."

No way, I'm thinking.

What age is he now? Might still be at school.

He's not the tiny kid he was when I first saw him, that's for sure. He's no giant, but he's shot up. Still not tall ... but neat swivel hips, strong legs... He *looks* more the part now ... no more Pinocchio in football shorts.

Still a schoolboy, but if they're good enough, they're old enough. And I need players, don't I? I might be able to use him ... next year, if not this. If I hold on to my job with Boro that is, and there has to be a question mark over that.

This year is probably out... Maybe not. Difficult to know. You put a kid on the field in the Conference, and he can get knocked about if he hasn't got the body strength. The Conference is no kids' league and it's not the Dog and Duck either. It's full of hard pros and semi-pros who are fit and know the ropes. They can dish it out. Could I put a youngster like him out for Hollins and Parborough, even if he is good enough?

The answer is yes.

I start talking to him. Lots of young players get setbacks. The game is full of players who were turned away by the big clubs ... years later they buy them for millions.

All this is going on in my head ... and he's got a wooden face on. He's walking back to the dressing rooms and I'm tailing along behind him, trying to talk, and all I'm getting is *grunt*.

I lead him into my personal sales-pitch: Wales, Everton, Leicester City, etc. In management now, at Hollins and Parborough, in the Conference. He's heard of Boro, just about. But he doesn't show any interest.

I plough on. "Boro are on the way up," I tell him – against all the evidence in the league table. "You might have seen Boro on Sky last year," I say – neglecting to add that Boro got done 5–1 by Northwich Victoria the one time they were on under the old management.

By now, I have convinced myself that I want him. It would be a risk – he's young – but he's better than anything I have in the team already. All it needs is a bit of work on his part ... if he still wants to be a player.

And if he does want to be a player, there's no reason why he should sign for me. The Os, Brentford, QPR, Barnet, Wycombe are all on his doorstep, even if the Premiership clubs don't want him. He's only got to go knocking, and they'd give him a trial. Not to mention the non-leaguers.

If he's sane, he won't sign for a club like Boro when there must be others who would at least take a look at him.

But he *might*. He just might.

I might get this kid who has the kind of class that belongs at Arsenal or Liverpool or Man U in my team, on my pitch, and he might just work miracles for me. And I need someone to do it, because the lads I've got aren't going to.

"Not on anyone's books now, are you?" I say, making it sound casual.

Wrong thing to say. He doesn't even want to think about whatever happened to him at White Hart Lane.

"Look," he says, dismissively, as we stop outside the dressing rooms. "It's over. I don't play no more. Not for real. Over and out."

And I sense the time has come to pull back.

"Well, if you ever change your mind, give me a call," I say, retreating. I leave him with my name and number, and I get his details, though I have to force them out of him. I'm not leaving without them, not passing this chance up.

Then I did what you do in the game.

I got on the phone to old Bob Lambetter, who used to be goalkeeping coach when I was at Derby County, before he left them for the Canaries. Never a top-rank keeper, but he'd worked himself into a nice little number on the coaching staff at White Hart Lane after he left Carrow Road.

Bob's job was with the keepers, but he was a contact at Tottenham and the only inside pull I had with them. I reckoned he would know what the background story was.

So I ring him, ding-a-ling, and we have a long chat, because Bob is a serial football gossip, first class. And a good man.

I dropped it in, trying to sound casual.

"Bob," I said. "I've been looking at a kid – Matt Jezz, Buzzer? Remember him? You had him at the Lane a few years ago. Played wide on the left against my young lads at Town just after you went to Tottenham. Under age, but lots of promise?"

Bob remembered him all right. I could hear the regret in his voice.

"Didn't make it," Bob told me. "Ray Clinton spent time on him – a good prospect, we all thought. Then Buzz got hurt in a pre-season game. And he was out ... what, most of a season, more maybe? Then he comes back too soon, and he can't quite do it. Then another injury. Three ... four months out, and he has to start all over again, picking up the pieces. Next he catches some bug – jaundice or some viral infection. One of the ones that does you in. We nurse him back, don't rush him, but by the time he's fit, the others have left him behind, and his head goes down. He's supposed to move up a grade, and at the end of the season we can't move him. Nice little lad ... but they reckoned he wasn't going to make it for us."

"In the head?" I asked.

"Yeah. His head. He's not believing, is

he?" Bob said. "When he comes back from the jaundice, or whatever it was, he's playing like he doesn't think he can do it. So he stops trying. And it gets into his game, so even the bread-and-butter balls we get them playing on the training pitch are beyond him. What can you do? We've a lot of kids here competing for places. Ray and I gave him all the chances we could, but there was nothing for it in the end. We had no room for him. He had to go. Disappointing, though ... seeing a talented kid like that going nowhere."

"Yes," I said.

"I rated him," Bob said defiantly. "Still do. But Ray thought he'd had enough chances."

"Ray Clinton's not infallible," I said. "Nobody is."

"That's it," Bob said. "Even the Pope makes mistakes."

"Spurs blew it with him ... is that what you're saying?"

"I'm saying I know we were wrong to release him," Bob said. "I hollered at the time, but no one would listen. I reckon the boy has the potential to make it, if someone gives him a chance. You take a long hard look, Mickey, because there aren't many like him. The verdict here was that he was an *if only*, young Jezz. We all knew he could do it, if only he would..."

"Yes?" I said.

"He's worth working on," Bob said. "Seriously. I reckon it's still in him ... must be. Maybe all he needs is a new start somewhere else. Go for it, Mickey. I would if I had the say-so."

So that's it. What Bob is telling me is, *Sign him*.

I'm on. I'm going to sign him. I'll have this superkid in a Boro shirt if it kills me.

I ring off after a bit more chat about this and that, and a lead about a young keeper called Connor, ex-Luton Town. Spurs had had a tip-off on the grapevine that he was useful, and Bob took a look. But they're overloaded with keepers already at the Lane, and the decision has gone against him. This sounds like a good lead to me, and I thank Bob, because I badly need a keeper.

You've got it, of course.

My *double*-lucky day, though I'd no way of knowing it then.

Bob's young keeper turned out to be Zack Connor, but then he was just another little-boy-lost from Dublin, who'd been shown the door by Luton Town. To be fair to the coaches at Luton, Zack back then wasn't anything like the aggressive it's-my-box keeper he's become. They were probably justified in letting him go. It wasn't till Andy Miller took him in hand that Zack really got a grip on the keeping job.

But that's another story ... I hadn't even seen Zack play then.

It was Buzz I was concentrating on.

I'm having my dinner and my head is so full up I could burst, going over what's happened as I chew my tandoori chicken. I've found a kid who is special, slumming in a Dog and Duck. The backroom boy's dream – finding someone the rest of the game has missed. And I'm not getting on the line to my contacts at Orient or Torquay or Bournemouth, tipping them off about Jezz... Not this time. Not for beer money, which is all I would get.

I've got Hollins and Parborough to think of. It's *my* team, *my* neck on the block if the chopper comes down.

Boro comes first. Young as he is, I've convinced myself that a not-fully-grown Buzzer can do a job for me at Conference level.

If I can get him match-fit, turn things round in his head, make him believe in his game again, he could change things round for my team ... and prove that Tottenham were wrong, that he's not an *if only*.

All I've got to do is find the switch that turns Buzzer's footballing head back on, and flick it.

MANAGER'S WEDNESDAY SELECT
v ALAN JACK'S

SEVEN-A-SIDE PRACTICE MATCH

VENUE: THE BACK PATCH AT HOLLINS AND

PARBOROUGH STADIUM, MANOR

LANE, PARBOROUGH, SURREY

Buzz has played at a lot of important places: Anfield, Highbury, the Bridge, Old Trafford, St James' Park ... all the great English stadia. He's a big game player. So why include a seven-a-side practice match on the car park behind the grandstand at Hollins and Parborough in his story?

Here's the background.

Getting Buzz on Boro's books wasn't as difficult as I'd thought it might be, given his history and his disenchantment with the game.

He's still a schoolboy and wet behind the ears, so it's the mum and dad I have to win round. And the good news is they are up for it.

That I'm not expecting. I don't have to woo them. My turning up is something they have been hoping would happen.

"You give it a go," they tell a reluctant Buzzer. "Show Tottenham they were wrong."

And before I know what is happening, I have him, all square and above board. No backhanders, no flowers and chocolates for Mum, no days at the races for Dad-Jezz. I haven't got it to give, and they aren't asking for it.

Mind, it wasn't all plain sailing.

I'm getting to know the side roads around Shepherd's Bush, chasing him.

"We're worried about Matt," his dad tells me, after I've been to their house and signed him up.

"Don't fret," I tell the man. "I'll look after him."

"Matt has never been the same since Spurs showed him the door," Dad-Jezz says. "What with the jaundice, then that ... Matt's been moping round ever since. There was a bit of a music thing – him and his mates trying to get up a band in somebody's garage. Came to nothing. There's been a girlfriend or two, but they didn't stick. Teachers got onto us – worried about him. They say he has a lot of ability, but he doesn't seem to get it together at school."

Well, we've all felt that way, haven't we?

Me, I couldn't leave school quickly enough. All I stayed around for was the football.

Which is how I wound up the football fanatic I am.

That's it then, sorted.

His dad's retreating to the house – good mover, light on his feet – and I'm about to start up the car, and I look up.

Matt – Buzz to you and me – is at the window, upstairs. He sees me looking, and I give him a wave, but he makes like he hasn't been looking, hasn't seen it.

Anxious, I reckon. The way Buzz reads it, I represent his Last Chance Saloon.

He's gone from Tottenham Hotspur down to Hollins and Parborough, from Ray Clinton and Bob Lambetter to me, and he knows in his heart of hearts that it is a long way back to where he could have been by now – should have been, in my book.

Truth is, when I get him down to the ground, he isn't an instant revelation, either. He's gone way, way back on the stamina, so we have to work him and work him – myself and Alan Jack, who's my back-up.

The skill's there – Buzz can do things on the ball better than anybody I have on the books at Boro – but the stamina and the upper-body strength are missing.

So we half kill him on training nights ... or Alan does. He's out there working Buzz extra, when the rest have long since quit and are in the showers.

Some of the others notice it, and already they are asking questions.

For all their shortcomings on the pitch, there are some world-class dressing-room egos here. Prima donnas wouldn't be in it. They're playing low league and low wage, and the evidence may be against most of them, but they're still hoping – thinking one day it will come right and their names will be in the paper. In their dreams, they're all the Pelés and Maradonas someone missed. Otherwise they wouldn't be out there breaking their backs in training for a few measly quid.

If we'd brought in an ex-international with a reputation in the game – earning the kind of money we couldn't remotely afford on our wage bill – they'd have taken it on the chin, and whoever was left on the bench would have been able to live with it.

That's one thing... The idea that a school-kid might come in from nowhere and take your place is something entirely different.

The cold fact is that if and when I put Buzz *in* ... somebody else has to be *out*.

I've got two or three youngsters, but the bulk of the Boro team is a lot older than I'd like it to be – old pros on the way out and a few youngsters on short-term loan from league teams to make up the number. A warning light is flashing in my brain. I could find the dressing room turning against me if I don't handle this right.

I have a talk with Alan about it, and from then on he makes sure he comes down rough on Buzz in front of the others. That way, the boy will avoid the nasty stuff that can go with with the tag of manager's pet.

"You want to do it in the game, you got to put something extra in," Alan bawls at him. "Can't play you till you're good and ready, son."

Alan is a hard man. He's doing Mr Nasty, making Buzz work.

Me, I'm doing Mr Nice.

The lucky thing is, he's still young, so we can start him quietly in the youth team Alan runs in the local Sunday league – give him a few games, get the juices flowing, make sure he's up for it before we try him with the pros.

Alan's Sunday side are not bad, and some of the opposition is better than you'd expect – certainly not Dog and Duck, but not Buzz's class either. All we're asking is that he eases himself in, gets back in the game.

What Buzz needs is a bit of success, and he comes on quickly.

Alan's still slagging him off, up front, for the pros' benefit, but behind doors he's crowing to me.

Buzz done this. Buzz done that. Alan's glowing about him.

I'm feeling good. You get a kid like that sometimes, who isn't the finished article. You think he's going places, but no one else can see it, so maybe you've got it wrong.

But here I have Alan telling me I'm *right* ... and Alan's been there. He's been a useful player – Woking, spells at Plymouth Argyle and Bristol City, then a good run at Wycombe Wanderers. He's had six clubs in fifteen years, and he's still there when I need him – player-coach with the seconds, capable of a run in the first team if there are injuries and we need him to play. He's slow, but he reads the game well, and nobody comes up against him without knowing they've been in a game.

So there we are.

Buzz is going well, and we've got to decide if we can put him on the team. Whoever gets left out isn't going to like it, is he? Players have mates, and they talk a lot, and a grumble can become a dressing-room revolution. So we have to handle it carefully, myself and Alan.

Of course ... if he comes in and plays *well*, then they'll clamour to have Buzz in the side.

Players are like that. They want results ... badly.

They'll put up with anything if scorelines

start turning in their favour. If we're going to use him, we have to have the dressing room *wanting* him in the team.

We need the older players seeing what *we* see in the kid, so they'll beg us to put him in and so we can get a few results together.

As things turned out, it was a routine Wednesday seven-a-side which worked the trick for Buzz.

The way the pros have seen him up to now, he's the new kid on the block, who has hit a good patch for the youth team, and might get a look-in for the seconds, late season.

There's been a downpour that Wednesday, so all we have used in training is the running track round the pitch, and the gym. Afterwards some of them – the keener ones – clamour for their usual bit on the ball. We tell them they can have a kick-about round the back, in the old mud-patch car park.

It's getting late and visibility's bad ... but they need the ball, don't they?

It's a seven-a-side kick-about behind the south stand, under the lights we use for car parking.

This is the young lads from our Sunday-morning team against Alan and some of his elderly mates from the second team.

And Alan is going hard on the youngsters, particularly Buzz.

"Time you met some real opposition!" he tells the kid. "No holds barred."

And he's slagging Buzz off as too soft for the game.

He lifts Buzz once … twice… And I'm watching, and I see what he's doing.

He gets the kid riled, and suddenly Buzz is turning it on, like something important has gone click in him, linking his feet with his brain.

Buzz isn't playing one-two touch and pass any more … which by rights he's supposed to be doing. Instead he has it in for Mr Nasty, and he's show-boating, playing the angles, exposing Alan's limitations.

He's twisting and turning, and making Alan look what he is – old meat.

He turns Alan inside, stops, shields the ball, twists him outside again, then in, then out… And Alan winds up swiping at Buzz, missing, and landing on his backside in a puddle.

Alan is howling abuse at him, and the kid is grinning and giving back as good as he gets.

I like it. I really like it.

The game gets serious … because the other players catch on to what is happening, and they see their coach is being made to look like a dumbo, and they like it.

Lads always like that.

Alan's running Buzz now, pushing him, shoving him. Some of what's happening is outside the laws, but Alan has the whistle round his neck, so it's not going to get blown, is it?

Buzz takes all Alan can give and comes back with more of his own stuff from his little book of magic.

He's gliding past old Alan, and he's laying the ball off, making space so he can get it back again – which isn't so easy on a tiny, muddy pitch.

And he's showing us the whole bag of tricks.

It's in-out-all-turn-about, and the lads are slagging Alan off and cheering Buzz every time he goes past the old defender.

Alan has no chance.

Neither does the keeper – who is Zack Connor. I'd picked up on Bob Lambetter's recommendation. One game in the Stiffs and I'd seen enough. Zack was straight into the first team – Luton Town's loss, my gain, thanks to Bob.

Buzz put three past him, and even then Zack was no slouch, though he hadn't learnt his trade. He was a shot-stopper, like so many young keepers. The command wasn't there. What he needed was what we hadn't got – someone who could take him out there and show him the ropes.

It's all know-how ... goalkeeping. You learn that. OK ... so Zack wasn't what he is now, but the raw talent was there.

And he didn't like being beaten. Buzz's first is a tap-in. Zack can do nothing about it – Buzz has ghosted in from nowhere.

The next is a neat bit of footwork on the ball that draws young Zack onto him. Then he nutmegs the keeper, which means they're all laughing at Zack, aren't they?

"I'll get you for that!" Zack tells him. The goalie's covered in mud, and the rain is dripping off the end of his nose, and he's beginning to lose it.

The third is a volley from halfway down the tiny pitch.

Zack sees it whistle past him.

The good news is the way Buzz hit it: the full Buzzer thing – power and accuracy.

Now they're all slagging Zack off, and Zack is insisting that the car-park lights are so dim that he couldn't see the ball until it was past him. He would have saved it in a proper match.

"You'll never do that again!" he tells Buzz.

Funny thing is, Buzz never has. Zack has managed clean sheets against Buzz ever since. Must be seven or eight games, nine if you include the England v Ireland so-called friendly at Lansdowne Road when Buzz came on in the second half. There aren't many keepers in the country who have a record like that against Buzz.

The bad news is that Alan's car is parked round the back, just off the car park, behind the two oil drums we're using as posts.

He has the car there with the headlights switched on, to make the pitch a bit brighter.

Buzz's thunderbolt hits the car door and bangs off it into the side wall.

"You little sod! You bust my car door!" Alan yells at him. Up to then he has been putting it on, working on Buzz to get him going. Now he has really lost it.

And it's true about the car. There's a big dent in the metal. It's an eight-year-old Astra, but still...

There's steam coming out of Alan's ears, and he takes his little bobble hat and throws it at Buzz. Buzz picks up the hat. Then he picks up the ball, and sticks a glob of mud on it. Next he sticks the hat on top of the ball.

He hands the ball with the hat on back to Alan.

"Present for you, Boss," he says, grinning.

That's the end of the game. A wet Alan takes off after Buzz, slinging mud, and everyone else is off after him, and they're yelling and laughing and egging Alan on...

And I'm loving it.

LOVING IT ... capital letters.

Because the kid is back, isn't he? He's

brimful of what he can do, and the others have seen it.

Alan's seven included five who were in and out of the first team and knew the ropes. That night there wasn't one of them could get near Buzz.

He was ghosting around like some player from another planet – which he is, only nobody knew that then. This was only a kick-about, wasn't it? He was putting his heart and soul into it because of Alan's mind games, but some of the others were just having a lark.

The old pros knew.

Some of the senior players have been watching, and by now they are looking at each other and wondering, because they know that what this *Buzz* has done is not something they're going to see every day, is it?

It's the something special you get when a player like Buzz turns it on. You don't forget that, once you've seen it.

I talked to Bob Lambetter about that practice game, long afterwards. He says Jimmy Greaves was like that in his early days at the Bridge, before he went to Spurs. Not in my time, of course. But according to Bob, the place used to light up when Jimmy got on the ball. Chelsea had a decent side then: Bobby Smith and Les Allen – England class – and then there was Greavsie – Greavsie out there, snaking his way through every time, nicking goals when there were no goals to nick.

That's the sort of talent Buzz has shown us, lighting up that night in the seven-a-side at Hollins and Parborough. The players are telling themselves, *Buzz is a natural.*

"That's it," Alan says to me. "It's clicked. Now we need to get him in a real game to see if he can do it where it counts."

"You're starting Saturday for the seconds against Kingstonian. You show Alan you can do it," I tell young Matt.

The kid drinks it in.

He's getting his first real competitive game with the pros. He's in dreamland. He's grinning at Alan, and I'm thanking my stars I've got a guy like Alan around, who knows how to handle kids.

I reckon we're going places.

We'll get Buzz into the first team, get him up front, banging a few in.

It's what Boro need – a goalscorer. What team doesn't? If we get Buzz up to the mark, we might manage a few results in the league and get a run in one of the cups. After that, who knows what might happen?

That night I'm thinking maybe my next football move won't be downwards after all. I could find myself managing in the league, instead of propping up the Conference. I'm rolling the oil drums back off the car park when the players have gone. I'm pushing these oil drums with Alan, and we're both sopping wet and muddy and happy, the pair of us.

Good night, that was. OK, so it didn't all turn out the way I'd hoped for Alan or me, but it came right in the nick of time for Buzzer ... and we were part of it.

BORO v KINGSTONIAN

RESERVE GAME

VENUE: HOLLINS AND PARBOROUGH STADIUM,

MANOR LANE, PARBOROUGH, SURREY

Alan knew the kid had it. And Alan worked him. Alan's been a central defender all his life. He's played against some of the best. There's nothing about the game that Alan doesn't know.

"I'd do this to you if you do that," Alan's telling Buzz. "I'd do that to you if you do this." And he's getting through into Jezz's brain – that's good, because the Sunday youth-team opposition isn't that hot. Alan's telling him he'll have it tougher when he's up against know-how.

The irony of it was, when we fast-track him onto the field for the reserves against Kingstonian, what he comes up against isn't an Alan Jack, but a no-brain, no-hoper like

Sam King. *Made for Buzz*, Alan and I thought when we saw their team sheet before the game. *The kid will take him apart, no bother*.

Then I'm looking at Alan, and Alan is looking at me.

"He fancies himself as a hard man, Sam does," Alan tells me.

Sam's going to jostle him, trip him, nail him – flailing elbows, jump tackles, the lot.

So we're going to find out if the kid can take it, aren't we?

How will Buzz react when Sam clobbers him … *which we reckon he will*?

How will Sam react when Buzz skins him … *which we also reckon he will*?

If Buzz can't cope with Sam, who is all huff and puff and no class, he's never going to cope with the real thing when he comes up against it.

The only negative is we can't use him the way we really want him, as a striker, because we reckon he hasn't the size for it at this level.

How wrong can you be!

"His natural position is up front," Bob Lambetter tells me, in one of his, by now, regular phone calls. Bob likes to keep tabs on what's going on, because we have signed his two recommendations – Buzz and Zack.

"Well, we're tucking him in midfield, working forward when he can – because of his size," I tell Bob.

"Let him lead the line, I would," Bob keeps insisting. "Make full use of his pace."

But it's my team, not Bob's. I listen, but I handle the Buzz business my own way, though I talk things over with Alan that night.

"No way young Matt starts up front!" Alan says. "Maybe later, but up front now he could get knocked about. They have one or two dinosaurs at the back."

"Sam King will knock him about anyway," I tell Alan.

"Yes … if he can catch him!" Alan grins back "You're running this team, Mickey, not Bob. What you've been telling me all week is what you should do. Stick with it."

So we go with the original plan.

We put Buzz in the midfield, with instructions to work forward behind our front two but not to neglect his defensive duties either. He was an attacking midfielder, but definitely a midfielder, not wide left going forward, where Alan has been using him Sundays, or up front, where Bob says he should be.

We have to test him some time, and this is it. Let's face it, this is the reserves – they aren't that good or they wouldn't be playing second-team games for a middling Conference side. In the first team, where he might struggle to begin with, we'll ease Buzz in more if we have to. There's a big gap to hop over when you go up from the reserves at Conference level – don't kid yourself about that.

Buzz has to show us what he can do first.

The plus of our long injury list, as far as Buzz is concerned, is that we've had to draft Alan into the team. So he'll be there on the pitch, talking Buzz through the game. We reckon we can keep him working, see how he lasts the pace of the game.

They've a few old soldiers dropping down from the Kingstonian first team out there, but nothing we can't cope with. The year before we did them 3–1 at their place, and they didn't like it.

Especially the aforementioned Sam King.

Dirty little brute, with a list of reds and yellows against his name, and a reputation for lipping the opposition. All knees and arms and elbows when he wades in – the positional sense of a baboon. Energy, stamina and no brain.

We're talking relative standards here. Sam's a part-time pro. Put him or his like in any park team anywhere and he'll win the game for you, scare the pants off whoever he comes up against. Move him up a grade and he'll give all he's got, but he'll struggle to hold his place in Kingstonian's seconds, and he's got very little chance of making their Conference side.

"Listen," I tell Alan. "Don't you protect young Buzz too much. He's not out there to be protected. If he gets settled in and survives the first ten minutes he'll be on full power."

That's what I'm hoping will happen.

And Sam must have read the script.

It is *yack, yack, yack* from Sam even as they line up. Straight from the kick-off he's after Buzz – bundling him, kicking, and hacking away round his ankles. It's raining like there's never been rain before, and the pitch is a quagmire, and before Buzz knows what is happening to him, he's bundled head over tip off the ball.

Free kick to us.

Sam isn't concerned. He's made his point, hasn't he?

The next time Sam gets close to him, Buzz has just taken an easy lay-off from Alan. He's holding the ball, looking for someone to play it to, just inside the centre circle.

Sam goes sliding in from the back, in the mud, two-footed – nearly kills Buzz.

Whistle should have gone again, but it didn't. The ref's allowing for the conditions, maybe. Or maybe he's green and doesn't know what he's doing.

A player like Sam can wreck a good game. Sometimes he intimidates the ref as much as the other team. Then the whole game turns sour, and everybody kicks everybody. The other way,

Sam gets booked early, and that sets the standard. If you're unlucky, the ref finds himself carding someone else soon afterwards, and the players begin to worry about being sent off or suspended. Then you get a niggly whistle-game which never opens up.

This game, we reckon the ref lost it early, using the conditions as an excuse. Either that or he's swallowed his whistle ... because he's letting a lot of stuff go that should be penalized. Sam must be thinking it's his day. He can rough our boy up, and the ref's going to let it go.

Buzz gets back on his feet, and Sam's up his back – *yack, yack, yack* at him, nudging him in the back, tugging at his shirt.

Ball doesn't go anywhere near them, but as they turn to follow the play, Buzz is down again.

What did Sam do?

Don't know. Didn't see it.

That's Sam's game in a nutshell. On or off the ball, he's going to impose himself.

Buzz gets up, looking disgusted. Alan yells at him, gestures.

Then there's a long ball down the middle. Kingstonian know it's Alan. They know Alan can't run the way he used to. They are trying to catch him, make him move about, get the ball in behind him.

Alan is too old a warhorse for that.

He gets up above his man. Flick of the head and the ball drops neatly at Buzz's feet. Buzz controls, seems to hesitate.

In comes Sam, crunching, elbows flying.

Sam thinks the hesitation Buzz is showing is down to the roughhousing he's already had, and Sam reckons that's a good sign – he's got Buzz the way he wants him.

But Sam's wrong ... *spectacularly* wrong.

Buzz taps the ball sideways as the tackle comes in.

It's one of those beautiful moments that you live for.

Sam's slithering in, studs up ... and Buzz isn't there. He's jumped the tackle. Lovely. And the tackle that was meant to take Buzz out takes out the ref instead. Sam goes scything in and the ref goes down in a bundle on top of him. He winds up sliding off Sam's back, with Sam down in the mud.

Meanwhile, Buzz takes off like a rocket.

He is headed inside and Nicky Bap is outside him. Buzz slide-rules Nicky in and goes past his defender, and Nicky plays it back, and Buzz hits it.

Misses.

He's hit it from way out, and the goalkeeper is nowhere. The ball clips the top of the bar and goes out for a goal kick.

No goal that time.

But it wasn't long coming.

Buzz has gone electric. He's turning Sam inside and out, spraying the ball round him, and we're on top of the game. We have young Grant filling in up front for us, and Grant has intelligence, so he's combining well with Buzz. Not made for the job, Grant, but we have our usual crisis with injuries, and Grant is a kid who nods his head when you ask him to play anywhere. He's just glad to be in the team.

It's going well.

Buzz has the ball wide right, where he's gone roaming – not in the book of defensive instructions we read him before the game, but that's what he's done.

Buzz stops on the ball – he's made himself the time and space to do that – looks up, and the pass is on. He plays it long over the heads of the defenders to young Grant.

It's a pinpoint ball, taking their stopper out, but just short of a ball the keeper can come off his line and claim.

All Grant has to do is nod it past the keeper … and he does.

So we're 1–0 in front.

Grant is a happy, happy boy!

But you have to spot it, don't you? And there aren't many at this level who can do that and deliver the ball the way Buzz just has. The vision thing – either a kid has it, or he hasn't.

It is unstoppable, a goal like that, made in some footballing heaven.

That's why young Grant is hugging Buzz, 'cause he knows the goal was a gift.

We've put Buzz in to come from behind and score goals, and he's showing us he can deliver for the others as well.

Then we're 2–0, when Sam up-ends Bobby Myrhe in the area. Alan slots it in. Could have let Buzz hit it, I reckon, let the kid get his name on the score sheet in his début for the Stiffs ... but he didn't. Player-coach's privilege. And I reckon Alan likes to see his name on the score sheet.

"What if he'd stepped up and thumped it straight at the keeper?" Alan said to me later, excusing himself. "Great if he'd scored. But missing a spot kick early on in the game is no way to start out."

Saying that now, when Buzz has such a name for dead-ball situations, sounds odd. But that was then. Now, he's known for his nerve ... then, it hadn't been tested.

He got himself on the score sheet anyway.

Not one of his spectacular specials, but special in its own way, just the same, for what it showed us.

Corner kick. The ball floats in.

Alan's up there and gets his head on the ball, near post. Flicks it on over everybody, and there's our kid on the back post. Sam –

63

who should have been on him – has gone walkies in his usual Sam style and Buzz is leaping like a salmon, then jackknifing his body so he gets the full power of his neck into it.

3–0 to us.

The ball ripples down the back of the net.

The big thing isn't the header, though it was good. The big thing is that he was where he was – he'd found himself space right on top of the goal, where there shouldn't be any.

You can show kids how they *should* do that, but you can't *make* them do it in the heat of a game.

It's the Lineker thing. The Law thing. The Michael Owen thing. The goal-sniffer thing. Being there when the ball drops.

They *do* it. *How* they do it, I don't know.

Buzz is delighted with himself … and so he should be – goal on his début for the reserves.

Arms in the air, handsprings, somersault! Then he's on his way back to the centre circle, arms raised.

By this time, Sam has been chasing all over the park without getting even close to Buzz's shadow. He's been tricked, and turned, and dumped on his backside, and now Buzz has lost him in the box and scored with a header.

Sam has had it for the day.

Running after Buzz on his way back to the

centre circle, Sam flicks him with the boot ... right in front of the ref.

Buzz is down. Ref has to have seen it this time.

Sam is OFF! Red-carded straight off. No yellow. Even this ref couldn't let that one go.

The Kingstonian coaches on the bench are livid with Sam. Nobody likes to see stuff like that. Their coach Dickie Laterby says as much to me later. They're a good club, decent standards. And the game's not about thirty-year-old apes beating up kids, even if they have been turned inside out and made to look rubbish.

By the sound of the songs the Kingstonian boys are singing on the bench, Sam won't be with them much longer.

After that...

Well, there's not a lot after that.

3–0 down at half-time, down to ten men, and Kingstonian have lost the plot.

There is a brief rally at the start of the second half.

They get one back because young Beanpole Hunter stays on his line when he should have come out and cut the cross off. They're geed up by that ... but they're wary about throwing too much forward because of Buzz and his pace.

By this time Buzz has more or less forgotten he's supposed to have any midfield defensive duties. We're up against ten men. There's space in the middle. He's got his goal. He's up for it, and he's gone a-wandering, despite Alan's protestations from the back. Every time Buzz can get forward with the front two, he does. And more often than not he's in front of them ... basically because he's thinking so quickly that they can't match him. He sees an opportunity ... and he's on his way.

Lovely.

We're not worried by what's happening. Because he's worth it, isn't he? Time for the lessons about discipline later. For now, he has Kingstonian going bananas trying to cope. They're ringing the changes at the back, but there's no one there who can live with him.

Mostly, he's doing things the easy way. He just shoves it past them and goes. Even when they're coming forward, they're thinking, *Lose the ball and that little bit of light will be on it.*

It's nice that – seeing the opposition lose the game in their heads because there's a talent out there they can't deal with.

That's the big bit, for me.

We knew he had pace – we've seen it in the youth games, and in training. We knew he had control. Now we're seeing pace and control against a not-half-bad side, and he's showing us an awareness of what's happening around him – more than we had ever dreamt of – because the instinct for position has clicked in as well, hasn't it?

Again and again, he's where he ought to be – out of the box and in it. Going forward, that is. Defensively, he's a no-show, but you can't blame the kid, can you? Not when the ball is running for him, and he's on his game. In those circumstances you pack up the coaching stuff and go with the flow.

He's ripping them apart. It's party-time.

4–1 to us ... Grant again.

5–1 ... Buzz, a clip with no back-lift. Inside the box, but it came off a sliced clearance on the line. He'd no time to think about it. He just did it.

"You did all right," Alan tells him when they're trudging off. "But it won't always be like that, and you've got to learn a bit about when you go forward and when you don't. We covered for you ... but you left a lot of gaps."

"Yeah," Buzz says. "Yeah, I know."

And just for a moment his face clouds over. Then he grins, a great big dirty grin. His face is streaked with mud and sweat, and I'm thinking, *He's back. Now he knows he can do it.*

And then Sam's coming towards him, suddenly, from nowhere.

And I move, and Alan moves, but the ape is there before us. Not going to pick a fight, is he?

No.

Shakes Buzzer's hand.

"Brilliant, kid!" Sam says, beaming. And the way he says it, you can see he means it.

Strange lot, footballers. He's spent all afternoon roughhousing Buzz, been shown up, finally lost it and got sent off ... but he's *seen one,* hasn't he? Bloke like Sam, tearaway on the pitch, never made it, never going to make it, probably going to get his marching orders ... still, he loves it when he sees the real thing.

He'll be on cloud nine these days, in some pub somewhere, now Buzzer has his name in lights. Every time Buzz is on TV strutting his stuff, Sam will be sitting up straight on his bar stool, boasting to his mates, *Played against him when I was at Kingstonian!*

Big moment in his small career, probably. One he'll tell his grandchildren about ... though he might just forget to mention getting sent off ... and what he was red-carded for.

Jezz's dad is there too. He is drenched to the skin, and he has a Moscow hat, complete with ear-flaps. He's down from the stand and leaning over the railing, and he's hugging Buzz.

"Wait till I tell your mum about this, Matt!" he says.

68

And he floats off home in his wellington boots and his hat, like a man who has just begun to see a dream come true.

It's not just Dad-Jezz I'm pleased for.

It's me, and Alan. We've found one!

BORO v FOREST GREEN

CONFERENCE

VENUE: HOLLINS AND PARBOROUGH STADIUM,

MANOR LANE, PARBOROUGH, SURREY

Our home game against Forest Green marked Buzz's full début in the Conference, after a handful of appearances as a sub.

The Boro team Alan and I had inherited that year was struggling. We operated on a shoestring budget, in a Conference season dominated by Yeovil Town and Dagenham and Redbridge, who had broken well clear of the pack after the first half-dozen games.

It wasn't all bad – I'd pulled a few strokes.

Zack Connor was one, though he was still learning the job. He'd come into the team and kept his place with some encouraging performances behind a defence that was always struggling. It wasn't a good introduction for a young keeper learning his trade, but he did well.

I'd also brought in Steve Larkin.

Steve had been a centre-back who didn't make the cut at Gillingham. I changed him round, put him up front, and it worked. Steve turned out to be brilliant for us, but it meant that we had someone still learning his trade leading the line. We started the season with the veteran Stan Pereson working off him. Stan knew the ropes, and he was helping Steve, but basically the two of them were feeding off scraps.

Not conceding goals was the early message – which it always is when the results are going against you. We told the lads they had to join the hard-to-beat club, and they took it on board. This gave us a defensive bias. We hadn't got anyone creative in midfield, and Steve and Stan were often left isolated up front.

Then, with the season hardly started, Stan Pereson broke his leg making a no-hope challenge in the game against Hereford and we brought in Bobby Myrhe from the reserves. He started well, but he got hurt when we lost to Yeovil.

We're left with one striker who had a season of first-team experience – Gogo Johnson – then Steve Larkin, Buzz and play-anywhere Grant.

By this time, we regard Buzz as a viable

option coming from behind the main two, but not up front in his own right … and only coming on towards the end of games, because we don't know if he can last the ninety. We have been pushing him as much as we can, but Alan is still against risking him as an out-and-out striker in the first team.

Bob Lambetter takes the opposite line in his telephone calls.

"Give him a run in the team. See what he can do!" Bob urges me.

"Put Buzz up front too soon and we could spoil all we've been trying to do with him," Alan is moaning, when we talk about it later.

We're slipping down the table, we're dropping points like confetti, *and* we're running out of players.

"Your job is on the line. So is mine!" I tell him. "We have to change things around."

It comes to a shouting match between us – not the only one we ever had, but this is one I'm going to win, because I'm the manager.

Bad as things are, we don't just throw him in. We have him on the bench, and initially he doesn't set the world on fire when he does play.

Ten minutes against Leigh RMI… Doesn't show much.

The same – or much the same – at Altrincham, and Rovers, where he links well with

72

Larkin ... which is encouraging.

He's making progress, but not as fast as we need him to.

For one thing, he's still developing stamina. He plays in bursts, and doesn't look as if he can offer the full ninety minutes yet, or anything like it.

For another thing, a lot of the drills he was used to at the Lane aren't happening around him ... or if they do, they happen more slowly than he's expecting them to.

The quick little triangles he had with Bower, the nuts and bolts of changing possession into attack, don't work out for him because Boro are way behind his mind-speed. That simple, quick, play-the-ball-the-way-you-are-facing interchange relies on the player you give the ball to being able to control it or play it on one-touch – which is why one-touch is such an important part of the game.

Buzz is laying little square balls to guys who haven't the ability to give-and-go that he's used to. They mishit the return, or they dwell on the ball and get caught, or they wallop it long when he's moved short.

It happens too often with Buzz ... not because he's laying off bad balls, but because the others either can't read him or haven't the ability to play the ball on where he wants it.

Alan is lecturing him about it ... and about his work rate.

"You've got to play in the team you're in," he tells Buzz, "not some wonder-team in your own mind. You've got to give them more time to think, 'cause they'll never get it right otherwise. And if you do lay it off and lose it, then you've got to get back and cover the mistake, whether losing it is your fault or not."

It comes to a head against Chester City at our place. We're losing, so I take the plunge. I go with the three of them together in that last fifteen minutes – Buzz, Steve Larkin and Gogo Johnson – all-out attack.

From 2–0 down, we manage to lose it 3–2, and the fact that we make a fight of it at the finish has a lot to do with the way Steve and Buzz are going at the Chester defence.

I'm praising Buzz, but Alan has a different message.

From Alan's point of view, their third goal is down to Buzz, because in the last few minutes, with everybody back behind the ball, he's tried to play a difficult diagonal ball out of defence, when he should have hoofed it into Row Z. The outcome is that we concede a goal through losing possession in a dangerous area.

"That's another point down the tube. We would have held out for the draw if it hadn't been for you. Your responsibility!" Alan yells at Buzz after the game. "You're not out there to indulge your own game, Matt. You've got to work it for the team. Down here, that means no fancy-pants lay-offs. Get rid of the ball when you have to."

Alan is out of order, but it's his will to win that sets him slagging Buzz off – that and the fact that when things go wrong Alan can see the danger, but he hasn't got the pace to cut it any more. Alan shouldn't be in the team, but we have so many early season injuries that he has to play. He's seeing the consequence of Buzz's mistakes from the receiving end, not from the comfort of the dug-out where he should be.

Buzz plainly doesn't understand why Alan is giving him grief, and he shows it. He's getting conflicting messages about what he's supposed to do on the ball – *Use it* and *Clear your lines.*

At training, Alan is dinning it into him that he has to express himself and play his own game. Then, when he tries to do it on the field, Alan is saying the opposite at top volume with a string of curses – *Get rid of the ball...*

It's not all bad. Larkin keeps scoring. He's a bit hit-and-miss, but he's a willing lad, and he keeps going ... that's Larkin. Gogo has also had some chances. The wavelength they're on doesn't extend to getting the ball back from Steve or Gogo when Buzz has made his runs. Larkin has learnt to lay the ball off properly now, but he hadn't then. And Gogo is just Gogo. Get the ball and he go-goes, but not very far, usually.

Still, put all three of them in the same team and there's goals. That's the message.

And we have to try him for the ninety sometime, don't we?

So ... we go for it.

We're leaking goals any road. Let's see if we can stick the three of them up front together, and score some ourselves. It cuts across the idea of playing Buzz midfield coming forward, but we have to try something else, and it has to be sooner rather than later if we're going to save our season. We're still in the FA Cup. Make it to the third round, draw a big club, and we could still end up with smiling faces in the boardroom.

We give Buzz his full Conference début against Forest Green at our place.

"You go out and play it your own way!" we tell him. "Bomb on behind the front two, get forward. See if you can link up with Steve and Gogo and turn things around for us."

It's a dangerous gambit, but with injuries and bad results we've run out of options, so we might as well go for broke.

Weighing it up coming into the match, Alan and I think it's a game that could suit Buzz. That season, Forest Green are not near the top, but they're not near the bottom either. They're a decent side and there are no crunchers in there. There's also a lack of pace about their back four. Decent team. Home game.

So it looks good.

If all goes well, we decide we'll give him sixty or seventy minutes to make an impact. Then we'll look at it, and maybe take him off and bring the more defensively-minded Grant on.

The odd thing is that Buzz's full début in the Conference pans out as almost the same story as his début for the reserves. Then, it was his personal duel with Sam King that decided the game. This time, he's up against a very different kind of player in Davie Titcher, but again the game revolves around the way these two handle each other.

The coaching manuals tell you that football is a team game, which it is, of course. But often a game can turn on the one-on-one confrontations that are going on round the pitch. If you get on top in one area, that dominance can spread right across the park, and you find yourself winning games that you might have expected to lose.

So this turns out to be one of those one-on-one games, and Buzz, in his new free role linking up with the front two, is the focus of it, just as we'd hoped he would be.

This team is much, much better than anything he's come up against before. Davie Titcher has real class and know-how – even if he is thirty-eight years old and long past his best days, when he played for Wolves and Scotland. He *is* the Forest Green defence. They count on him to hold the fort for them at the back every week, and every week he does it – the kind of inspirational player you'd give your eye teeth to have in your team at this level.

"If he does Davie, we'll know he's OK," I tell Alan.

"Nobody does Davie," Alan says.

"OK," I say. "If Davie does him, it will be a useful learning curve for the lad, won't it?"

Alan just shakes his head.

"Look," I tell him. "Davie's dropped down the leagues, he's playing from memory, and almost as slow as you are. Buzz has pace. He'll burn the old guy off."

"You watch Davie," Alan says. "I saw him play Ryan Giggs back when Davie was with Coventry. Giggsy hardly got a look-in."

"Giggsy must have had an off day then," I tell him. "Anyway, how long ago was that? Davie is a set-up for the knacker's yard these days – he'd never see Giggsy going past him, and he won't catch Buzz, either!"

That's how confident I'm sounding, trying to talk Alan round ... and keeping my fingers crossed.

Davie hasn't the pace any more, but he has brain and experience. Within ten minutes of kick-off he has spotted the role we've given Buzz, and he delegates himself to snuff Buzz out. The battle royal with Larkin that he'd come into the game expecting he leaves to his mates at the back.

Immediately, he's blocking, and niggling at Buzzer, and that makes the kid do a bit more.

It's a one-on-one duel.

"Take him on! Take him on!" I'm yelling at Buzzer.

And he does. He starts doing what he can do but hasn't shown us often enough. It isn't just push-past-and-run. He's coming good all in a rush, and our game's revolving around him.

Already Davie has his hands on his hips, taking a breather, and he's yelling at the others around him for cover, trying to pull things about so they'll cut off the supply of the ball to Buzz. Our lads are finding Buzz. His link-up play has come on in leaps and bounds, and he's drifting all over, finding Steve and Gogo when he can, and then coming through for the lay-offs – well, Steve's lay-offs anyhow, Gogo doesn't do them, generally speaking.

Buzz comes off Davie again and again, dragging him out of the middle with deep runs on the flanks, like I told him to, making those old legs work. And Davie rises to the occasion. He takes Buzz twice in quick succession, sets things up on our goal ... but each time it snuffs out, and we have the ball again, and it goes to Buzz, because Buzz is the one who is moving.

Buzz does Davie wide right. Then he does him again, cutting in.

Then they have a one-on-one chase down the middle after a through-ball from the back, which Davie just manages to turn for a corner, more by luck than judgement.

Buzz is showing us the real stuff – a kind of cross between Georgie Best, Jimmy Greaves and Ryan Giggs. Low-slung body makes him nifty, quick on the turn, so he spins round and he's off.

He's won the battle, hasn't he? Davie can't cope. Something has to give for Forest Green ... and it almost does.

Buzz feints and shuffles – surreal stuff, all twinkle feet – sprays the ball far wide, pinball pass, beautiful, takes two men out, puts Grant clear. Grant pings it back inside, first touch, and now Buzz is clear himself. He takes the ball in his stride, screws it back across the face of the goal for Steve Larkin to come onto ... and the goalie makes a blinding save.

If Larkin could finish half the chances he finds he'd be a real star. As it is, he is what he is. He never really moved on, Larkin, in a footballing sense. Still basically a bull, although several managers have thought they could make more of him. He's made a name for himself now, after that big-game hat-trick he got at Villa Park in the Cup semi. Still, he was – and *is* – a willing worker when he has good players round him: players like Buzz, and Jed Armstrong when he went to Villa. He'll always try. He'll miss more than he scores. But he's honest, and he gives you everything. He can make things happen for you when he's on song. You've got to credit the lad with that.

Back to the game, and the real talent – Buzzer.

Our boy has a solo run on goal, beats three men, smacks it against a post; it comes out and Gogo Johnson balloons it wide ... again.

We're still 0–0, and we need the points. Someone has to put it in the net. Buzz feeds Larkin in twice ... and Stevie misses twice. Stevie's applauding the passes, and he has his head up, because he figures there's more to come.

Buzzer's everywhere, calling for the ball, taking people on, making his runs. Davie's yacking at the players around him. He knows he needs help, but help isn't forthcoming, because our game has perked up. Buzz has set us a standard, and suddenly, three or four of ours switch on. Even Gogo has started play-ing football.

This is a game that is going our way. We've taken a risk with young Matt Jezz, and it's coming off big time. They're not hurting us, and we don't need the extra man at the back. All we need is for Stevie to get on the end of one and stick it in.

Then we get the breakthrough we've been waiting for ... and it's Buzz. It had to be, with the way he's been playing, and the way Larkin's been consistently missing.

Buzz does it the easy way ... for him. He's broken through on the edge of the box. Two men closing on him. *He'll be the meat in the sandwich*, I'm thinking. *They'll bring him down. Penalty.*

No way. Buzz shuffles between them, side-steps another, drills it – one of Buzzer's best – low to the far corner. The keeper is left looking a pillock.

1–0 to us.

Then he gets another chance to put us further in front.

Nothing too complicated. Bad marking, but he uses his brain again. Dead-ball situation, and old Jon Ireton is on the ball, wide left, signalling what he wants done. When he gets on the field – which isn't often because of his dodgy fitness – old Jon bosses the free kicks. Wouldn't have been in the team if we hadn't a long line of injuries, but we have, in spades. So Jon's back in the shirt, and he's making the most of his swan song, revelling in it.

He lines up the ball with another player as a decoy, but we know Jon is going to hit it. We know that, and probably they know that too ... only they can't be certain, can they?

Larkin has drifted near post, taking his man with him – he always does that well.

Alan has come up from the back, like he always does for the dead-ball situations. He may not be able to run, but Alan still has the ability to mix it in the opposition's box, and if he gets a header on goal, it is usually there, or thereabouts.

Alan's lying edge of the box, right-hand side, ready for a diagonal run which will hopefully take him across in front of his marker. If Jon misses out Larkin, Alan should be on it, we're thinking. That's the variation we've worked out on the blackboard.

Jezz is lined up alongside Alan, as Jon takes the kick. Jon could go for the gap at the end of the wall ... or he could drift it to Alan's head. And the defence read it wrong. Three defenders all go the one way, reading it as an Alan ball.

But it isn't.

Alan makes his run near post, joining Larkin, but Buzz has pulled out, taking Davie with him. Then Buzz turns and darts forward, far post, into the space his move has created, quick as light. This isn't part of any pre-arranged plan, just the kind of brilliant variation that changes games, if you have a player who can come up with it.

Jon doesn't pick out Alan or go for the gap at the end of the wall.

Instead, he spots Buzz's move and plays it to him.

Buzz has got clear of Davie and is powering in all alone on the far post.

He doesn't connect cleanly because he gets the ball and the keeper in the same moment, and they go down in a tangle, but Buzz has got something or other on it, and the ball cannons off the keeper onto the post and comes back to Larkin, who bundles it into the net.

Stevie's got his goal and he's a happy boy.

Scrappy-old mucky-old shin-in goal, but it counts.

2–0.

We're at the end of our losing streak. It's coming good. Looks like the risk of playing three players whose mindset is dominated by the idea of going forward has worked for us.

Smallest player on the pitch, and Buzz found himself a free spot in a goal-mouth melee, and a goal resulted.

The bad news is that young Matt is flattened doing it.

Full fist on the jaw. Nothing deliberate about it, but the keeper has flailed out, trying to reach the ball as they tangled, before the ball broke free to Larkin.

I'm thinking, *It would happen*. At long last Buzz is starting to turn on what he can really do, and he gets clobbered. Now we'll be back to square one again.

We take him to the line and his face is starting to swell.

I'm asking him if he wants to stay off.

The look on his face – there's no way he'll stay off. That's what I'm wanting to see.

He's back on. And suddenly, the banana lip from the keeper's blow means nothing – he's back swaggering and turning it on, and he's in and out and everywhere.

Davie doesn't give up. Every twist, every turn, Davie is bothering him, following him ... and it ends up the same each time. Jezz does him for pace. That's because Davie is thirty-eight years old. Ten years earlier, in his Coventry/Wolves days, Davie might have lived with Buzzer. Now, it's no contest.

The rest of that half is a masterclass. Our whole team are coming forward, all over Forest Green.

Buzz has two more breaks: a dipper from the edge of the area that no one else would have attempted but that just clips the bar and goes wide, and a smart one-two that takes him to the angle of the box, where he chips it onto Stevie's head.

All Stevie has to do is nod it home, which he does, thus ensuring it will be his name in the paper, not Buzz's. That suits us well enough. The press always go for the goal-scorers. It takes them more time to pick up on where the chances are coming from.

The crowd are going, *Stevie–Stevie–Stevie*, and Larkin milks it like mad.

3–0 to us.

Alan's grinning all over his face at half-time, giving me the thumbs up.

All those weeks getting battered about at the back, and suddenly we're attacking, and we're winning. It's working. Alan and me, we're in clover.

The second half, Buzz is good, but not as good as before. The steam has gone out of his little legs and Davie has got his second wind. He's got an old pro's stamina, has Davie.

Buzz put him through the shredder first half, but this half, the old guy is more than holding his own. He's arranged things so the others double up for him marking Buzz, when he needs help.

And Davie whacks Buzz once or twice, just to let him know he's there. Nothing vicious about it; well within the laws of the game.

Still, we've seen plenty. We've got more out of Buzz than we could possibly expect, and he's learnt a lot from the way Davie has set about him.

They go 3–1, scoring from a breakaway

when we're outnumbered at the back.

That switches them on.

We bring Gogo back to help, but it makes no difference.

Davie has left off marking Buzz, and switches himself into an attacking libero mode, feeding everybody around him.

In the end, we have to take Buzz back as well in a desperate attempt to cover the moves Davie is making, leaving Steve Larkin alone chasing long balls up front.

Buzz has his turn at trying to cut the old guy out, and he can't do it.

Davie doesn't wait around. He pushes it, moves, gets it returned, pushes it again, and he's dominating.

We have to sub Buzz for young Grant with fifteen to go, because we're just about hanging on, and we need the extra man in defence.

We are not up to it. They go 3–2 with eight minutes to go.

Then Zack Connor misreads a cross, comes out, knows he's lost it, stops, stranded halfway out of goal.

Alan gets back, clears it off the line.

And that's it... We hang on to 3–2. We're hoping we've turned the corner. Maybe we can rewrite the script for the rest of the season.

Best of all – using Buzz up front has done it for us.

87

"Not bad," I tell young Matt. "You're coming on."

He's sitting there in the dressing room, whacked, with a grin on his face despite the big bruise and the banana lip that is ruining his good looks. He knows he's played a blinder, even if he couldn't hold out at the end. So he can't help the grin, can he?

Me, I don't blame him. If I'd managed what he managed for even half a game in the whole of my career I'd have been singing all the way home on the team bus.

"Who's the new Georgie Best?" Davie Titcher asks me after the game. "He looks like he'd break in two if you touched him … if you could get near enough to touch him, that is. He did me every time he got the ball. Like trying to catch a little wriggly eel. Something different, isn't he?"

"Yeah! Different!" I tell him. "Still, you coped, Davie. He hardly got a kick second half."

"Did, didn't I?" Davie says, pleased with himself. "But it wasn't down to me, was it? He'd put so much into that first half, he was bound to lose a bit later. I paced myself. Your kid didn't. I'm surprised you didn't sub him earlier on."

"Seriously, what do you reckon, David?" Alan asks him respectfully. "You've been around. We want him in the team, and he's improving every game he plays. But he's a bit of a liability when we haven't got the ball, and he can't stay the full ninety minutes. Do we go for it, and give him a run in the team when we have the others back fit again, or don't we?"

"Depends how long you reckon you'll have him for," Davie says, sharply enough. "He goes on like that, one of the big clubs is going to come asking. Then you've lost him anyway, haven't you?"

And that's the big question. If Buzzer goes on improving, we'll lose him to someone in Division One or the Premiership, sure as eggs is eggs.

Boro are five points clear of the relegation teams, but there are still plenty of points to play for. We've both been in teams that lost their way, Alan and myself, and we don't want it happening to Boro when we're in charge.

Then we have the FA Cup game against Dover Town coming up. It's a game which might just save our managerial bacon ... if we win it. And *if* we draw a big fish in round three.

BORO v MILLWALL

FA CUP THIRD ROUND

VENUE: HOLLINS AND PARBOROUGH STADIUM,

MANOR LANE, PARBOROUGH, SURREY

We made it through to the third round, winning against Dover Town, but Buzz didn't feature in the game. A thigh strain the week before put paid to that.

We'd persevered, as planned, with the three-up-front line-out using young Buzz in the games leading up to the Cup game, and it went as well as we had any right to expect, given that we were still struggling with a long injury list.

Alan, for instance, was now a regular in the first team – something we hadn't envisaged when he joined the club. He was supposed to be looking after the youth side and filling in with the reserves when needed. But we had to play him in the first team ...

there just wasn't anybody else.

Buzz lasted the full ninety minutes in two of the three games before the Dover game, and scored three goals. The goals were nothing to tell your mother about. He didn't show us anything we hadn't seen already – except the knack of being there, getting on the end of stuff that other people don't.

You have that knack, or you haven't, and Matt did enough to convince us that he had it. Always *has* had it. Always will.

In general play, apart from the goals – if you can *ever* separate a striker's contribution to the game from his goals – he was easing his way in nicely, adjusting better to the players around him as he got to know their strengths and weaknesses.

That pleased us, because he was thinking for the team, not just himself, and he cut some of the over-elaboration which often flawed his play. Defensively, his game still left a lot to be desired, but his shortcomings in that respect had to be balanced against the exciting options he offered us going forward.

All this was good, but ... we still weren't getting results, and there was even more boardroom muttering than there had been before. We were a new combo. The season had only got going ... and already they were asking the wrong questions.

We reckoned we had to beat Dover Town

in the Cup, and get a glamour club in the third round, or Alan and I would be going walkies down to the job centre, clutching our P45s.

We're relying on Buzz to turn it on for us, and we wind up bust as usual, because, come match day, we have to go without Buzz. A minor knock in training put him out of contention – joining five other first team players on the injured list.

So we're sure we're out. Like they say on Sky, *sick as parrots*. We're on our way out of the cup, for sure. No third round for us.

Not so. The lads really played for us that day. We scraped through with a 1–0 victory, by virtue of Alan's headed goal in the thirteenth minute, following an in-swinging corner. It was a desperate rearguard action for the rest of the ninety minutes. Zack Connor excelled himself with a double penalty save in stoppage time: first blocking the spot kick and then somehow reaching the follow-up and turning the ball over the bar.

So we'd got a reprieve, hadn't we? The atmosphere at the club bucked up, and then the draw for the third round came through.

We wanted Man U at Old Trafford.

What we got was Millwall at our place.

Big enough to get us beat; not big enough to bring the Sky cameras down. Sod it!

The draw cooled the atmosphere in the dressing room, more than somewhat. Realistically, we were no-hopers against the Lions. They must have known it... We certainly did.

This is not what Alan and I are telling the lads.

We tell them, *It's prove ourselves time. Get some points in the league; get ourselves a few goals. Millwall won't know what has hit them.*

Fine. Sounded lovely at training. We almost believed it ourselves.

Then reality kicked in. We're still dropping points we should have taken, home and away, and leaking give-away goals ... particularly at Ramsgate, when young Zack plays with an injury and lets in three soft goals.

"At least we're consistent!" I tell Alan after that one.

"Yes. Consistent losers," he says.

Going into the third round of the Cup, we're bottom but five in the Conference. We kept telling ourselves and the players that we had matches in hand – which we had – but the threat of relegation was very real.

The ice is in the air coming out of the grille above the boardroom door. The chairman isn't speaking to us any more.

"If we do go down, you and I won't be here to see it," I tell Alan.

"Not going to happen!" he insists. "The lads will lift themselves for the Cup, won't they? Beat Millwall, get to the fourth round, and the confidence will come back and we'll get things rolling again. Watch this space."

So we're pinning everything on the game with Millwall.

How many men we got walking? was the first thought each Saturday morning, and the Saturday of the Millwall game was no different. Our dressing room was like a bleeding hospital.

We are short seven possibles – four of them regulars on the first team. We field the walking wounded. Alan goes into the game with his thigh strapped. Larkin has four stitches in his forehead and a head bandage that makes him look like something left over from Frankenstein. Young Zack still has his thigh strain and can just about play, though he has a problem with the dead ball. Nicky Bap has his right ankle strapped and is moaning and groaning.

We start with erratic Gogo and Steve Larkin up front, and Buzz in a free role behind them, which is about the only part of the team that is roughly the way we want. We have to play Grant in midfield, where older heads ought to be, with Bap from the seconds alongside. This is a serious weakness, but what can we do? We simply haven't the numbers. It was the story of our season: when we need our so-called big-game players … they aren't there.

It could have been different, if we'd been able to field a full side more than six times in the season. Now we'll never know if we could have made that squad into a team.

So we're fielding a side without several regulars, propped up with young kids like Grant, and old guys like Alan – player-coach all right, but he was supposed to be playing in the reserves, not a third round Cup tie – and Jon Ireton.

Millwall are … well, Millwall are Millwall.

I've worked there, and they still have four or five from my time. Good sound keeper in Bouncer Lewis, four-four-two, with Danziga and Whiteside big enough and quick enough to cause us all sorts of bother coming forward and old Clipper Hansen capable of wriggling his way down the flank, though he is several yards short of the pace he had in his Portsmouth and Chelsea days. They'd run us off the field on a good day, basically. Skate all round us … stroll it.

The Cup is different, we tell the lads. *One-off, at home, on our mud patch. You against them on the day.*

To Buzz we say, *You do it for us, son … please?*

We know he can do it, if he can drift out wide and get himself one-to-one with Clipper.

Going past the old guy should be a cakewalk, and Clipper doesn't get back much these days after he's beaten. We reckon Buzz can be the ace in the pack that undoes them for us, because they haven't come up against Buzz, have they? Of course, they've been down to our place coming up to the game to have a look, but the thing is, we've blown those games, haven't we? Nothing doing up front, only scraps. They've seen Larkin can score goals, but they've not seen much of what Buzz can do ... not the real Buzz, when he's on song, injury-free.

That's what we're hoping anyway.

Kick-off, and there's a wind blowing down the pitch towards our end, which will do us no favours. But we've lost the toss so we have to live with it.

The ball is ballooning about, straight from the kick-off. This Millwall team, packed with First Division experience and know-how comes at us ... and they're overhitting it. They just tap the ball and it's gone for a goal kick.

The only one trying to pass it is Clipper. The rest are going like tanks. Obviously they've come out with the idea that if they get two or three up by half-time, we'll be gone. They are thinking it's no contest.

Eight minutes gone, and we've hardly seen the ball. Gogo gets it wide, pushes it too far. Chick Melrose has closed him down and moves onto the ball.

As he moves, Chick slips. The ball breaks off him and suddenly Gogo is clear on goal.

Being Gogo and sensing that this is his glory day, he ignores Larkin, who had a tap in, and blasts it himself.

The shot is hit hard enough to beat most keepers, but it's low near post, and that's Bouncer Lewis's speciality. Out comes a leg; the ball hits it, flicks the post and goes for a corner.

Bouncer is going mad ... and meanwhile Chick Melrose hasn't got up. He's gone down on his ankle, and he's off. That upsets them, and we have a corner kick.

Something goes wrong with their marking. Must have ... because they've seen our routines.

It's an absolute rerun of the goal that Alan scored for us against Dover in the last round ... which they've seen. They know set pieces are just about our only chance. They know Alan comes up for them, and they know his reputation in the box.

So they have it sussed.

Gogo's corner starts off as an in-swinger, ends up as an out-swinger because of the wind. Bouncer has started confidently off his line for it, but they've let Steve Larkin free, and he comes from the blind spot off

Bouncer's shoulder, cutting across him.

And the wind gusts as Bouncer goes up to gather it.

Bouncer is up, flailing over Larkin's head at a ball that he's suddenly realized he isn't going to reach.

And Alan is coming in.

Doesn't miss those, does he? Not Alan.

We're 1–0 in front, with about ten minutes on the clock.

They *know* Alan does that. They've seen him do it against Dover in the Cup round-ups on TV, *and* they know his reputation ... and *still* no one picks him up.

The ball is in the back of their net and they're standing looking at each other, yelling at Bouncer, and he's yelling back about who was marking that so-and-so. Well, they're not using those words exactly – it's a bit more colourful.

We figure with Chick off and Marston coming on to replace him, they haven't sorted out who was supposed to be marking Alan. But they should have done – should have been part of their homework, keeping Alan out of it at set pieces.

Against all the odds going into the game, we're winning.

Alan's clapping and yelling, and our lads are lifted.

We're not only 1–0 up, but we get a chance

to go 2–0 directly afterwards.

Buzz outpaces Clipper for what must be the third or fourth time and fires in a low dipping cross between Bouncer and their defenders.

Bouncer goes for it with Larkin, Larkin gets a touch on it, and the ball goes just wide. Near miss ... should have been a goal. We would have been 2–0 up, and probably game over. But we aren't, and it isn't. Still, this time you can't fault Steve. He got himself in there.

They're coming back into the game, and Danziga and Whiteside are combining well, with Clipper moving about and dragging Buzz back with him. Buzz is going against instructions ... but it's understandable. Buzz is trying to work for the team, despite all we've dinned into him about staying forward and a free role.

Clipper is laying the ball off short and getting it back and playing the big two in. The truth is that Millwall's front men are too much for our patched-up defence and it's all down to last-ditch tackles by Alan, who is continually marshalling things for us at the back. Brilliant, old Alan was.

You can't buy what he has to offer.

Twice they get through – first Whiteside, and then Danziga – and each time Alan gets a foot in and breaks it up, but only just in time.

Then Clipper's on the ball. He shows it

to Buzz, who has drifted back to the edge of our area, where he isn't supposed to be. But what else can you expect when our defence is being run ragged? Buzz puts his foot in, and Clipper's past him and away. Grant comes across to take him out, and Clipper clips it on the far post.

It seems Alan has it covered, but the ball is spinning up in the air and the wind gusts, and instead of getting a clean contact Alan misheads it up in the air. Whiteside is roaring in for Millwall and brushes Alan aside as he's turning. Whiteside is clean through on goal, Zack Connor is off his goal-line and fifty–fifty to get it, but Alan is desperate to cover his mistake so he sticks his foot out from behind, and Whiteside is down, in the area.

Penalty.

Alan was last man, so the ref sends him off.

We're done! 1–0 up, and a penalty against us, and no Alan, and it's going to be 1–1 with them on top.

Clipper takes the spot kick. He tries to place it, and Zack gets a hand to it and turns it round the post.

Just what the kid needed after his bad game at Ramsgate. He gets up and he's limping triumphantly round his goal, filled with himself. Going to be his day ... and our day. *Only another sixty-five minutes to hold out*, is what I am thinking in the dug-out. 1–0 up, and down to ten men.

And we've no one to cover the middle.

It shows how desperate we are that we switch Simon Grant into the middle and bring Gogo back to cover for him. With Buzz working as deep as he is, that leaves only Steve Larkin up front, and Steve's chasing and harrying every time we get the ball into their half – a lost cause, though he keeps at it. Always gives you the full ninety minutes, Stevie.

For the next twenty minutes the ball is hardly out of our half, what with the wind, their numerical supremacy, Gogo's not having a clue and Grant's not being able to cope. They're coming at us and coming at us and now everybody is back.

Zack Connor saves us maybe three or four times. The keeper's playing out of his skin … and basically on one leg, because of the injury he's carrying.

For Millwall, Whiteside and Danziga are tearing our middle apart and doing everything right … except score.

We get to half-time still 1–0 up, and in the second half we have the wind behind us, blowing into their goal.

But our lads are knackered.

They've been covering and covering, everybody working back, but we haven't had the ball for more than four or five passes at any stage. Millwall must be in their dressing room saying, *No problem, second half.*

Even being against the wind might help them, because they've kept up the overplaying in their anxiety to get back at us. It has been long ball after long ball, raining in, and either the wind just carries them back to the keeper or they go for goal kicks. Clipper has been tearing out what is left of his hair.

"It won't be that way in the second half," I tell Alan. "They'll sort it out."

They'll feed Clipper, and Clipper will tear us apart.

We have to have a Plan B. We move things about.

We put Gogo tight on Clipper, to spoil him. Gogo's brief is to run him, jostle him, keep niggling at him. Don't let him play his pretty link-ups with the big two. We're just hoping Gogo keeps his head and doesn't throw in one of his characteristic tackles, because we could have another red card if he does. That's move one.

Move two is the surprise to everyone except me and Alan. We pull Larkin back into the back four, beside Grant.

The way we read it, they've been having it their own way with every high ball that comes in. And Larkin is strong in the air, isn't he? Plus, he's played centre-back at Gillingham – even if he did make a hash of things there. So he knows the defensive ropes ... or he ought to. Maybe he can stop the flick-ons from Danziga to Whiteside that have been causing us so much bother.

"That leaves you up front on your own," we tell young Matt. "And we mean up front. No coming back. You're going to be working all by yourself. Anything we get out of defence you're to be on it, right? The longer it goes, the more men they'll be pushing up, and there are bound to be gaps. That's built for someone with your pace. With them chasing the game, there's bound to be something going your way. Maybe only one chance ... but you've got to take it. Get us a second goal, and the game could be over."

Buzz nods.

"You start dropping back, and we'll take you off!" I tell him. Though who I think I'm going to put on his place, I don't know, and he doesn't ask.

That's the plan: hold them as long as we can, look for a breakaway ... hope maybe Buzz can produce something for us.

Forty-ninth minute.

Harmless ball in, Larkin rises to nod it clear and young Zack – who has had to come for everything in the air up to now because there's no Alan to do the job for him – comes for it too. Doesn't call.

Larkin is back-pedalling, doesn't know the

keeper is coming.

Zack Connor fists the ball *and* Stevie, and the ball bangs off Stevie into the net.

1–1 ... with forty minutes still to go.

And Larkin is out cold, from Zack's punch.

Stevie is off on the stretcher, and we bring on Cole Cayman, who is a youngster from Alan's Sunday team, switch Jon Ireton into the centre – a position for which he is too short, too fat and too slow – and hope for the best.

To be fair to the lads, the best is what we get.

Old Jon isn't what you could call a cultured midfielder, but he has a bit of brawn, and he manages to hold Danziga most of the time.

Grant starts playing out of his skin against Whiteside. He's a marvel.

Zack Connor is still doing miracles behind them. Gogo has managed to do a job on Clipper Hansen, though there's a lot of shirt-tugging and niggles going on, and we lose several free kicks where we don't want to lose them ... but that is Gogo, isn't it? He was never meant to be a defender.

So we're coping, more or less. But the game has swung decisively in Millwall's favour. Keep on coming at what is left of our makeshift defence and they should get two or three more, no problem.

They're coming at us again and again,

in waves.

Meanwhile, Buzz is an ornament, up front, alone.

He knows he's the only out ball we've got ... not that we're finding him. The wind gusting down the pitch from our end to theirs is too strong. When we do get in a clearance – which isn't often – it runs on to their keeper nine times out of ten ... only there weren't ten. Buzz can't have had more than half a dozen balls to chase up to the seventy minute mark.

It's fruitless and frustrating for Buzz, with nothing he can do but try to work himself positions for passes that never reach him. There's nothing more difficult in football than to keep doing that when your mind tells you the ball isn't going to come.

But he keeps at it.

Almost nothing he can get near, and he's working and working, chasing and chasing, hoping and hoping, when most kids would have put their hands on their hips and given up.

He's got to keep concentrating, because he knows there's only likely to be one chance, and if it comes, he has to take it.

Then it happens.

Grant gets a hack on the ball as he slithers on his backside towards the touchline in a tackle with Danziga.

It's a hopeless ball, but Buzz starts after it

as their covering man moves to clear. They have three men over at the back, and nobody sees any danger until it's too late.

The ball breaks badly off the defender and Buzz is on it, twenty yards out, and going for goal. He has such blistering pace in those legs that they're never going to catch him.

He slots it over the keeper's body and in off the bottom of the bar.

No miracle about it. No wonder goal. But a goal just the same.

The ball is nestling there in the back of the net, and we're 2–1 up, with fifteen minutes left, when we could have (and should have) been three or four down.

And we're in the fourth round. Get Man U at Old Trafford. Big money. Board happy. Maybe save my managerial skin.

"It is our day!" I tell Alan.

They go straight down the field. Danziga flicks on … Whiteside. Goal.

2–2.

Back to where we started. But we have only ten men, remember, and the run of the game is against us.

They keep coming. We keep running. We're holding out, and we're wondering how we can get through the last few minutes, when it comes, because some of our lads at the back must be exhausted.

With two minutes left, Gogo hacks Clipper

near the edge of the area – which he's been doing all the time anyway – and Clipper gets up, dusts himself down and does a Beckham on us.

Zack sees it coming late and he can't get up to it.

3–2. And we're O-U-T. Game over.

We've held out for three-quarters of the game with ten men against a top First Division team, got in front twice and they've done us, right at the end.

It's head-down time in the home dressing room, and there's nothing we can do to raise them. Our lads are gutted.

"Great game, Matt," I tell Buzz.

He's been out there, and he's killed himself all second half with no service at all, and when the one and only break happens, he's managed to get onto the ball and do the business.

Striker can't do better than that, can he? Kept his concentration. Mind focused on what he had to do. Players twice his age can't bring that off in a game like the one we'd just been through. But Buzz did.

He's sitting there with his boots off and he looks at me.

There are tears in his eyes. He's done. We're done. End of dream ... till next season.

Except that we still have a lot of games to play.

"What do we do, after that?" I ask Alan.

"How do we get them up for it, midweek?" Midweek we have Hayes, away, and we need points like we have never needed them before.

"Don't know," Alan says, which just about sums up the mess we are in.

Losing that FA Cup tie against Millwall was a big blow for me and Alan, for kids like Gogo and young Grant, and for poor old Jon Ireton, who saw all his faint hopes of glory in his last season fade away.

Not for Buzz. I reckon he came out of it stronger than he went in.

The battering he had taken when Spurs dumped him was well behind him now, and the long road to that World Cup game in Rio and all there's been since – that road was laid out on the map for Buzz, just waiting for him to walk down it.

Me, I still had a minor role to play. I was auditioning to be Buzz's map-reader, though I didn't know it at the time.

STRIPES v MANCHESTER UNITED

PRE-SEASON FRIENDLY

VENUE: THE EAST MIDLANDS ABADA

COMMUNITY STADIUM

A few weeks after our defeat at the hands of Millwall, Alan and I had our contracts abruptly terminated *by mutual consent*. With Boro's insolvency, we never got the compensation that was due to us... But that's another story.

After we left, Boro looked like narrowly holding on to their Conference place under caretaker manager Jimmy Cliff. But off the field financial pressures led to the resignation of the chairman, James Nation, who disappeared to Barbados (before the police moved in), taking most of the club's documentation with him.

Hollins and Parborough went into receivership, from which they did not recover. They owed money all round: to the Supporters' Association, the players, the Inland Revenue, even the lady who came in to wash the shirts. The resulting legal disputes left them as they are today – an unhappy footnote in Conference history.

What happened to the lads we'd been working with?

Zack Connor moved on to greater things, as it was always likely he would – Bob Lambetter had been right about him. It seemed like a toss-up between joining Preston North End or Watford till Colino Ravessi's name came up in the frame. It was Colino's first crack at management in the English game, and Zack signed for him, which was probably the best move he'll ever make.

Gogo Johnson had a short and glorious spell with Brentford and then faded into obscurity with the Os – always a trier, Gogo. Showed more for Brentford than he ever did for me, mind ... but then, their set-up suited him in a way that ours never did.

Young Simon Grant was signed by Northwich Victoria. Two years later he played a leading part in their FA Cup run. He was a good kid, who kept trying, and I was glad to see him get something back for all the effort he put into his game.

Alan Jack made a brief return to league football as a player up north with Stockport

County – he needed the money. Alan performed creditably for half a season, before being forced out of the game by injury problems – and that's the last I heard of him.

Me, I can spot a player. I can talk the talk. But I haven't got what Alan had. He could get inside their heads. And that's what he did with young Buzz when the kid first came to Boro.

You know what happened to Alan later?

Nothing.

His name has gone missing from the tabloid accounts of Buzz's early career. My name gets mentioned, Bob Lambetter gets his bit – and Erik Goethe, of course – but nobody mentions Alan Jack, who did more for young Matt than anyone else.

That leaves Buzz, and Steve Larkin – the two prospects Alan and I always rated as the best we had at Boro, along with Zack.

Buzz played only one more game for Boro after the Cup tie, and even then he had to be withdrawn at half-time, due to a recurrence of the injury which had hindered his progress that season.

If any of the big boys were interested, Matt's injury stopped them having a second look.

Steve Larkin lost his edge in a struggling team ... so no one came in for him either.

On my advice, Matt and Stevie left Boro at the end of the season, when it became clear that there was no money to meet the players' wages – as they were fully entitled to do. The kids had shown promise, so there was interest in one or two quarters, but not what I was hoping for on their behalf.

I don't want them going just anywhere, do I?

Also, not to beat about the bush, I have to earn a living in the game some way, don't I? It is that or join the dole queue, because after Boro went down the tubes there aren't many offers coming in for my services.

So I talk to them in June. I tell them to sit tight and sign nothing, to wait and see what Uncle Mickey can do – without telling them how precarious their Uncle Mickey's position in the game was just then, I admit.

Buzz's little dad went along with it, because I was his kid's saviour. I'd brought his Matt back from the footballing wilderness, and he trusted me. Steve Larkin ... well, Stevie had his problems, and I'd sorted what I could, so he owed me one. I'd turned him round from the mess-up he made at Gillingham.

I have contacts in the game, don't I? And I use them.

And the upshot is that before the new season begins I have Buzz and Larkin on trial at the Stripes, where Declan Brody has taken over. It looked like a good move to me at the time – Stripes being in the Second Division and widely tipped to go up. It was bound to be better for the boys than some of the Conference and lower division sides who came sniffing.

The downside is that Declan Brody is a devious bloke. I'd not have gone near him if it hadn't been for the fact that joining the Stripes looked like such a good move for my two... And like him personally or not, Declan's reputation as a manager was A1 in those days.

He'd been a striker with an eye for goal in his Everton days – like Buzz, a good ball-player, but tall and awkward. Towards the end of his career at Stoke City and Bradford he'd picked up a reputation for dishing it out when he had to. We never played in the same team, but we knocked bits off each other on the field ... admittedly when he was well over the hill. He had a good run after he retired: a spell as a youth coach at Middlesbrough, then as manager at Grimbsy when he got them into the play-offs. Now he was taking over from Stan Ormsby at the Stripes.

Big step-up for the boys, if they could do enough to get Declan Brody to sign them. That's what I told them.

Trust your Uncle Mickey, I tell them. *I'll get a double deal that will work for both of you.*

And Declan Brody is as good as his word.

He has the boys down for pre-season prep, and then he has a series of long talks with me ... because I want the deal to be right for the lads, don't I? And I'm not entirely sure I trust Brody.

But it is Division Two, and he is a new broom at the club, and the word is that he's making an impression and they're going places. It could be the right move at the right time. Coming into a team that looks like winning things is just what the lads need.

The upshot of all the talking is that we agree he'll give them both some kind of a run during a pre-season friendly against Manchester United down at the Abada – which was the Stripes' home ground then. He's promising me that if they show up well, he'll have a word with his chairman and then he'll be talking money. He's new in the job, and the chairman's blue-eyed boy, so he doesn't think there will be any bother ... *if* the boys do the business. He's got rid of half a dozen no-hopers left over from the previous regime, so he has slots to fill and I know he's busy shopping around.

Declan shows me some respect, but he also speaks to a few other people who know the Conference form, and on the whole he seems to be impressed by what he hears – though most of the interest he expresses is for Stevie.

"Young Matt is head and shoulders better

than my other boy," I tell him. "Brilliant prospect."

Brody just grins at me.

"We'll see. What I've heard is that he's in and out, doesn't last the ninety," he says. "Also, he's injury-prone. Could be a liability. I've got the usual problem. My chairman wants results this season, not next or the one after."

I'm thinking *injury-prone* and I'm not happy. Maybe he means that that's down to Alan and me pushing the kid too fast.

"I've been there," I tell him. "But Buzz is different ... a one-off."

"I need a look at both your boys in a proper game," he says. "If either of them is good enough, I'm interested."

That's fair enough by me.

I know Larkin is good enough for Division Two ... there aren't many who can hustle and bustle like Stevie. In a better team than Boro he would have been scoring more goals and attracting a lot of attention. What he's done since makes my point.

Brody only has my word to go on about Buzz, and because of the boy's size and age he regards Buzz as a prospect for next season or the one after, not someone who's going to get into the first team set-up. Getting automatic promotion is his brief, so his priority is players he can put in straight off if he needs to.

115

Which Buzz is, I tell him.

"Yes, Mickey," he says. "But you would say that, wouldn't you? And I can't use your name as a football expert to persuade my chairman, can I?"

This is a remark which takes the smile off my face. The stink about what happened at Boro was still very much in the news. Having a Football Association inquiry hanging over you is no recommendation in the game.

"Leave it out," I tell him.

"I'm doing you a favour even looking at your lads, all things considered," he tells me, rubbing it in.

I have another word with Buzz and Steve Larkin. I'm telling them: *You know the score here; the ball is at your feet; your careers could take off if you do the business; show Brody what you're made of and you could get placed at Stripes.*

The Man U game didn't turn out as I'd hoped. It was a washout as far as Buzz's prospects were concerned. So why include it here? Because it was the one time in my involvement with Buzz that he got it badly wrong in footballing and personal terms. He was intelligent, but still very much an immature kid – and he made a kid's mistake.

Brody has Manchester United – well, *a* Manchester United XI anyway – slumming down at Stripes in a pre-season warm-up. His fans are excited. He'll draw a good crowd with United, and he knows it.

This one counts, Brody tells the press. But this game is not quite as big a deal as he makes out to the press ... or his board of directors. He has contacts with Old Trafford, and he's used them to get United to come down to the Community Stadium on a wink-and-nod basis – but this is *a* Manchester United XI, not *the* Manchester United. You never really know what you'll get from the big fish on these occasions.

Brody will be using it to try out a few for the Stripes – including Buzz and Larkin – and seeing how his summer signings blend in.

But a friendly is a friendly is a friendly – both teams halfway through their pre-season, and not fully up to the mark, nobody wanting to get injured.

Stripes will get a good run out against top level opposition, get the supporters enthused, probably get beat but give the Reds a decent game, so everybody will be happy.

In my dreams I'm thinking Buzz might get himself noticed and the lads would wind up with United ... because I've signed nothing for Declan Brody yet, have I? That's a chance he's taking.

I reckon he's a United type of player, Buzz. And he's still only just out of short-pants, so they'll reckon they can shape him their way. Plus, he knows, of course, the Old Trafford reputation.

Buzz is very, very impressed … he sees the big time in front of him, and his name in lights. He's hungry for it – so hungry that he breaks the golden rule.

Nothing to do with his previous injury, but he gets a knock on the ankle in training, and it's nagging him. He doesn't tell me, and he doesn't tell Brody. Big mistake. This is a big game for him and he's geared up for it and he reckons he can get through – which makes him a silly boy, doesn't it?

So – a warm-up friendly. Nice day, good crowd, start of season. All hunky-dory. Doesn't work out the way we planned it.

Steve Larkin is just as nervy as Buzz, but, unlike Buzz, he isn't carrying an injury. He's up for it. Fighting for his place in a league side. Thinking he has the world at his feet. Straight from the kick-off he's doing his bull-in-a-china-shop, and he's chasing everything, throwing himself about, and trying to make bother. To be fair to him, that is what all Brody's boys are doing – running about like headless chickens, trying to impress the new boss.

All but Buzz, that is. Buzz isn't doing much – and I'm wondering *why*? The reason is the ankle knock, of course. He's got out on the field and he's tried a run or two in the first ten minutes, and he knows he's hurting.

So he should pull up and get off. But he doesn't.

Meanwhile Larkin's getting worse.

Brody's man on the field is Iceman, and Iceman's groaning inside when he sees what Larkin's doing. You can see it in his face. He's been at West Ham and Man City, and some of the Manchester United lads are his mates. They don't want kicking pre-season. They can do without it.

Iceman is trying to calm Larkin down right from the start, but Stevie isn't listening.

The centre-back Stevie's up against is a Spanish international with all the know-how that comes with experience. He's handled harder men than Stevie will ever be.

Larkin is full of go, niggling the Spaniard, nicking. Twenty minutes of this, and they're kicking each other, nudging, body-checking – when the ball is there, and when it isn't. And it spreads. *You kick us – we kick you*, is what happens. Shouldn't. The Man United bench don't want it that way any more than Brody does – it's them coming down a level, the way United see it. Their players are worth several million a leg more than Brody's, and legs can get broken.

Niggle, niggle, niggle.

In the middle of the niggle, Buzz does

just about the only thing he did all day. He gets the ball with his back to goal, and the big Spaniard is breathing down his neck.

And he turns the Spaniard, doesn't he? Beautiful. Skins him.

Going clear... Could go for goal, but instead he drifts the ball back across the face, and Larkin's there, and he prods it home! The Buzz–Steve combination back in business!

Stevie Larkin runs up the field with the ball in his hands, like it's his glory day.

I'm beaming and thumbs-upping Declan, but Brody just stands there with his face like stone. That's his image thing, isn't it? And image counts a lot with Brody.

Straight away United make it 1–1 with a neat move down the left.

Then they're 2–1 up, with Iceman cut out for pace, and a little Norwegian under-21 forward gives the keeper no chance with the shot.

By this time there's words going on.

OK, we – Stripes that is – started the rough stuff, mainly down to Steve Larkin and his antics. *We deserve it*, is what I am thinking. But the game has taken that kind of shape, and once that happens there's no stopping it.

Buzz is usually up for it. With the tackles flying, a kid with quick feet like he has can usually find the room to do some damage. But today it isn't happening. He's in the game now and then, in flashes, a few nice link-ups with Steve – but mainly he just isn't showing.

He's protecting the injury, but I don't know that. Neither does Declan Brody, who has been waiting to see this new Giggs or Georgie Best I've been telling him about, and who, so far, has seen nothing.

One breakaway down the left, and Buzz over-elaborates and loses it, when he could have passed.

A quick flick in a goal-mouth scramble that almost finds the net... *But he found the space to do it in*, I'm thinking.

Two or three good runs off the ball that make space for Stevie.

That's Buzz's contribution.

Meanwhile, around him, the mayhem continues. The United backroom don't like what they're seeing, judging by the music coming from the bench.

They're yelling at their own guys to tame it, and the message is starting to get across ... just.

Then, Iceman hits a long ball out of defence for Stripes.

It's an act of desperation, not a pass – Iceman should have done better – but Larkin's after it.

He goes for it, windmilling with his arms, and he catches his marker in the face with his elbow. The marker goes down like he's been hit by a tram. He's rolling about, making the most of it. The way Stevie sees it, the guy isn't hurt, he's play-acting. Stevie goes to him, screaming blue murder about faking it. Stevie nudges the guy with his boot. It's not a kick, nothing like ... but the next thing, someone has barged Stevie, and he's down, and there's a melee on the edge of their box.

That's it. The ref sorts it out. This is a friendly, so no one gets carded, but suddenly there's stuff going on all over the pitch again.

Take him off! I'm willing Brody, because this is not what I've planned for Steve Larkin. He's blown it, hasn't he?

Brody does nothing.

It gets horrendous. When push comes to shove, United are bigger and tougher than Brody's boys, and much better footballers – and they start teasing.

They go pretty-pretty – not allowing Stripes any of the football.

You want it, you're going to have to come and get it off us, is what they mean.

Which gets the Stripes lads all hot and bothered.

They're chasing shadows, and, if anything, it gets tougher.

It's 3–1 at half-time, and the Manchester United bench deliver the message to Brody's chairman, in no uncertain terms: *Tell your lads to tone it down, or the game's over. We're walking off.*

For young Buzzer, the light has gone out. He limps back to the dug-out after half-time, head down, pigeon-toed.

Brody has pulled him off. And the worst of it is … Brody was right. I know it has gone wrong, but I don't know why. I've built Buzz up as a firecracker pre-match, and he hasn't shown anything at all.

Both teams are looking sheepish at the start of the second half.

United have been given the message about teaching these apes a lesson with their skill, not their muscle.

They come out show-boating, but at least they've started going forward again, looking out for their own reputations. They are so much better equipped to do it than Declan's lot that it's almost embarrassing.

That's the bad news.

The good news is Stevie.

He gets another one with twenty minutes left, right against the run of play. Bustles his man, rounds him and slots it home. That makes it 3–2 to United.

Basically, Stevie's strength has done it.

Then it goes sour.

Stevie reckons he's on a hat-trick and he loses it completely. He's thumping and shoving and pushing and generally misbehaving.

The United coach is up off the bench and he's talking to Brody.

He's pointing at Steve, and yelling at Declan.

Brody shrugs and gives in. He brings Steve off and that's the end of his hat-trick hopes. The crowd gives Stevie a cheer and he is clapping his hands above his head coming off, milking it.

In anything but a friendly he would have been sent off in the first twenty minutes, and I reckon Declan's not going to go for indiscipline like that in his new line-up, even if the fans like it.

So ... not a good day ... is it?

Steve's thrown his chance away, and young Matt has blown it by playing when he wasn't fit – which I've found out about by this time.

I give Buzz a rollicking, but I'm still telling him, "Don't despair, there'll be somewhere else for you and Steve – *only don't you ever do that to me again, hiding the fact that you're carrying one, will you?*"

"OK, Mickey," Buzz tells me.

He's looking miserable. So he should. I don't even wait to see Brody after the game. I just head for the car park.

"Got to wait for Stevie," Buzz reminds me. I've run them over to the Stripes in the car, looking after them.

We wait for Larkin, but he doesn't show up. We're starving, so after a quarter of an hour or so, I send young Matt limping over to McDonald's for a Big Mac each.

Two burgers later and we are still waiting.

The car is smelling of burgers, and by this time I'm beginning to lose it. The kids have let me down, both of them – in different ways. I've sorted Buzz, but now I want to have a few sharp words with Stevie, don't I? I'm gunning for him, big time.

I take a walk back to the ground, but there's only the ground staff around.

It looks like they've all gone home.

In the end, I drive back with Buzz and drop him at his house.

Then I head for the pub.

Next day I ring Larkin's home, and his brother tells me that Stevie is signing up with Brody for the season, and that Brody is telling him he'll get his place.

"No, he's not signing," I tell Stevie's brother. "Not till I've talked to him."

"Well, I'll get him to ring you when he comes in," the brother says.

And I wait till the next day and he still hasn't answered my call, so I ring again, and it seems Stevie still isn't about. I'm beginning to lose patience. So I ring Declan Brody to check out what exactly is happening.

"What's this I hear about Steve Larkin signing for you?" I ask.

"Yes, I signed him," Brody tells me. "Good kid. Plenty of go in him – not like the other one. Your young Matt Jezz was a waste of space out there. You must have seen that yourself. Like I was told, he's an injury-prone fancy dan that doesn't last the ninety. Didn't last the first five minutes, if you ask me. He hasn't got it. But I can do something with Steve Larkin. He puts his heart and soul into it, doesn't he? I like a kid who can handle himself. Not afraid of big reputations. The way he waded into the United back four was something else. I can build on that."

I'm not believing what I'm hearing.

"What do you mean, you signed Stevie?" I said slowly. "You're not signing him till I've had a word."

"Making out that you're Steve's agent, are you?" Declan says, laughing down the phone at me. "I've already *signed* the kid on the dotted line, Mickey. You've no status in this deal at all. He's my player now. He's happy. I'm happy. Sounds like you're the only one who isn't. Thank you for the recommendation. That's all. Bye!" he says, and the phone goes dead.

It's not as if I was an official agent – nothing on paper. I trusted Stevie.

So I'm sick and sore at Steve Larkin.

I've seen him play since … sure. But maybe

126

now you'll understand why I don't rate Larkin as high as his goal-scoring record might suggest I should.

Larkin double-crossed me, and I can't forget it.

What do I do? How do I react?

Well, I never put anything Brody's way again, first off. Declan Brody is off my Christmas card list.

When Swindon beat them in the play-offs that year I was there, and I laughed my head off when Steve got sent off again – for the third time in a season. And they lost 3–1.

Larkin got the goal, mind you.

That was before he head-butted the linesman.

But what did I do about Buzz?

Pulled the best stroke of my career, that's what I did.

By Wednesday of the following week, young Buzz had moved on, signing Premiership forms for Erik Goethe's City, who were on the verge of the biggest success in the club's history, though no one knew that then.

Buzz was on his way.

ROTHERHAM UNITED v CITY

LEAGUE CUP, FOURTH ROUND
VENUE: MILLMOOR, ROTHERHAM

The next time Buzz takes the field for a key match he is in a different shirt – and almost a different world, in football terms. It's the League Cup fourth round, and he's turning out for one of the Premiership big boys – City.

So how did he get into a Premiership squad on the back of being released by a Conference club like Boro and failing a trial with Stripes, perpetual also-rans in the Second Division?

Contacts ... that's how. Sure, there are people in the game who will pull a fast one on you if they can, like Brody did to me. There are others who treat their friends decently. It always comes round – you scratch my back, and I'll scratch yours.

It must have seemed like miracle time to an ambitious Buzz – suddenly everything was going right for him. The boy had worked hard under Alan and me at Boro, but this was a big-time payback he can only have dreamt of.

Didn't seem like it, the day Stripes turned Buzz down.

For Buzz, it was hamburger and gloom in the car park with me, while Stevie was on his way ... minus Mickey Griff.

And what happens?

In come City. Erik Goethe's City. Third in the Premiership the previous year, and hotly tipped to go further.

And they're not saying, *Come down here and let us have a look at you*. They're saying, *Sign – we want you*. And the contract they're offering is much better than standard terms for a kid his age, with very limited experience in the pro game, and a history of injury.

At first, I couldn't figure out what had happened. I'm just thinking, *The boy's luck had to change, and it has*. Obviously City must have had someone watching him. It turned out that the good guy behind all this was Bob Lambetter. Bob had moved on to City after the reorganization at White Hart Lane, where he had been given his marching orders.

Spurs should have held on to Bob, shouldn't they? But it was all-change time ... and their loss was City's gain.

There's no truth in the loose talk in the game about Bob using Buzz as a calling card when he talked to Erik Goethe at City. But let's just say having a line on a kid no one else rated didn't spoil his chances either.

I'd have done the same in his shoes.

It's to Erik Goethe's credit that he didn't waste time once he'd signed Buzz. A series of good displays for the Academy sides capped by two goals against Chelsea, three at Portsmouth in September ... and Erik was all smiles when next he saw me. "Nice one, Mickey," he said. "I owe you one."

Erik knew what he had on his hands – a young player he had picked up for a song who could go straight into his first-team squad.

It was pat-on-the-back time for Bob in his new job.

Buzz ... Buzz responded as I hoped he would. He was back at the level where he belonged ... so why wouldn't he?

By mid-October, Buzz was in the first-team squad. He made it onto the bench against the lower lights like Bolton and Birmingham and Blackburn, without actually making it onto the field. He was drinking in the atmosphere, and raring to go. Erik and Bob were excited about him – but they couldn't afford to drop points by putting him in too early either, could they?

Under Erik Goethe they'd secured their first Champions League place by finishing third in the Premiership the previous year, behind Man U and Liverpool, but everyone knew it was going to be make or break for them this time round. Either they would sail on and take the Premiership title for the first time, or they would slip back down the table, as so many clubs had done before them.

It went right to the wire, didn't it?

Early into the season the usual suspects – Arsenal, Man U, Liverpool, Chelsea, Newcastle and City – had all taken points off each other, and dropped points against teams they should have beaten. City were well up with the pace, only three points behind the leaders, Arsenal, coming into November. They were grabbing all the points that were going against the lower orders, giving nothing away to the middle to top, and holding their own with the big three. Twelve games undefeated, after Manchester City turned them over on day one – just about the only blip on Erik Goethe's record that season, because Manchester City were going nowhere.

"Listen," Erik told his players. "Put on a run, get the results we know we can get. This is our year."

And he had the players. City were a great squad that year.

From Buzz's viewpoint all this is fine …

but it's a settled squad, and they're winning points, and nobody seems to be picking up suspensions or long-term injuries. The only changes are tactical ones, or when someone needs a rest. They're all eager to play – because they know if they sit one out they might never get back in the team, don't they?

"I'm number six in the pecking order up front, Mickey," young Matt is moaning at me down the telephone. "And Erik and Bob keep saying I'm OK, I'll get in when the time is right. They say they don't want to push me too fast. They're working on my fitness, building me up. But the papers are on about them signing an extra striker. There's always a whisper about who they'll sign. What happens to me if they do that?"

"I'll talk to Bob," I tell him.

I've been nosing about, and there's a chance of a short-term loan to Palace, which would give the boy the experience he so badly needs.

Bob nods, talks it over with Erik.

The word comes back that Erik is comfortable with things as they are.

Ilya Sashka has fitness problems, two of the other strikers have been picking up yellow cards ... and, anyway, he wants to keep Buzz around the first-team set-up.

"Erik's working on him," Bob assures me. "It's personal with him now – he's got his own ideas about how to handle the kid's future. Doesn't want to rush him."

There's an implied dig at me and Alan there, but I let it go. We didn't rush Buzz – we just gave him a chance. What else could we do, with the way things panned out at Boro?

"Yeah, well ... who am I to contradict Erik?" I tell him, doubtfully.

"Erik's the best in the business when it comes to handling a kid like Buzz," Bob tells me. "He'll get his chance sooner or later, with the way things are going for us. What does the kid expect? Matt is way, way up, being where he is at his age. He may yet *have* to come in if things go against us, but, basically, Erik's view is he's for next year, maybe the one after that. Buzz is still very raw – he needs more time."

And I tell Buzz, and I soften it a little.

"You're nearly there," I say. "Just be patient. They respect you. You'll get your chance."

Two weeks later Buzz is on the phone to me again, and I'm talking to Bob again. This time it's Shrewsbury who have come asking. No chance. So it goes on.

Meanwhile City keep winning. If they go top, they might stay there and win the Premiership. So the spotlight is on them, and the pressure is on Erik to keep them up for it. Not a situation where he's going to put a kid in ... unless he has to.

"What do you want me to do?" Bob asks me. "Tell Erik to rest Ilya Sashka or Bobov and bring your boy in? You must be kidding."

The best I can do is tell Matt there'll be injuries, there'll be suspensions … stick around and his time will come. I'm telling him and I'm telling the little dad and Buzz's mum, and they're telling Buzz too … and he's still fretting.

Which, I tell him, is just how I want him to be.

Wanting it.

I tell him so – repeatedly – when he rings me. I'm not hands-on with Buzz now – can't afford to be. I have a living to make, and I'm making it with some difficulty: background colour jobs for the tabloids, the odd TV and radio appearance, a touch of the corporate hospitality lark. Basically, I do what I can to keep going – plus some scouting on the side.

Buzz calls me at least once a week. I'm still his mate, as far as the boy is concerned, and he knows I have my finger on the pulse … and his interests at heart.

Buzz's chance came at last in the League Cup, against Rotherham United, at Millmoor. The icing on the cake for me was that Rotherham had just taken on a new manager – my old boss from my days at Town, Teddy Maher, in another of his I-can-save-this-club forays.

Erik and Bob do what I'd do if I was them – though nobody likes it.

They put the fringe team out, don't they?

"Show us what you can do, lads!" they tell them.

Buzz is picked to play alongside Ilya Sashka, who has been struggling to regain his form since his injury in the Champions League Group B game against Porto. His early goal in that game meant that City topped their group, ahead of Juventus.

This Rotherham game is a tale of two strikers.

There's Buzz, making his first-team début in what is really a back-up scrap selection, and desperate to make an impression to further his career with City.

And there's Ilya Sashka.

Real Madrid, Benfica, Barcelona, Inter. Aged 36; coming off the back of a spell where he's playing with a niggling back injury; number three or number four in the pecking order, instead of the regular number one man he used to be.

The fans may still be on his side as well, but there are others in form, and he's not always as fit as he'd like to be... So he's slipping out of the picture, slowly, and he doesn't want to let himself down, does he? Doesn't want to be second fiddle, playing twenty minutes at the end of the game if they've gone behind.

It was Ilya Sashka's last season in the game, though nobody knew that then...

OK, the opposition isn't up to much. Good professional team, Rotherham, as always. And they're up for it. And they have a bit of twinkle at the front, in McPerson and Frail. But it's never going to be their night.

Not with Ilya Sashka doing his stuff the way he used to for Real Madrid.

And the beauty of it, from my point of view, is that he's not show-boating. He's working for the team. He knows he hasn't got the pace and Buzz has, so he switches on his footballing brain and sees that Buzz gets the right ball delivered at the right place and the right time so that together they can take the Rotherham defence apart.

That's the easy way to win this game, and he goes for it. Maybe Bob and Erik told him to go that way – or maybe that's just Ilya Sashka. But whatever instructions he was given, out on the park he is everywhere, play-ing those pinpoint flicks, those through balls that Buzz needs. Narrow pitch at Millmoor, but the way Sashka uses the ball creates spaces everywhere.

He makes Buzz look good ... and when you think about it, you know that he's *handing on* the glory, isn't he? Because the better Buzz looks in this game, the better Buzz's chances of making the first team – and that could be at Ilya's expense, couldn't it? So what Ilya Sashka is doing is writing a script that could signal the end of his own chances.

Five minutes in, and Ilya lays on the first one for Buzz.

The ball comes to him, edge of the box, played up from the back.

He takes it on the chest, controls it ... flips it right over his marker as he sees Buzz powering in.

Buzz takes it round the keeper and walks it into the net.

He's dancing, doing his thing, and Ilya is there with him, hugging the kid, ruffling his hair, and Buzz pats the old guy on his crew-cut head.

1–0 to City.

Two minutes later, Ilya Sashka plays a little cushioned header on the edge of the box, down to Buzz's feet.

It's a chance, but only a half-chance, because Buzz still had a defender coming at him.

This isn't the little Matt Jezz I had at Boro. This is the *Buzz* they've been working on. He's got a lot of strength in his upper body, and as the defender moves he leans into the challenge and takes it, which is an art in itself. Then he's away, over the outstretched leg – penalty if the Rotherham boot had caught him – and then the keeper is on his way, but no hope there because Buzz just dinks it over him.

2–0 to City.

The next big Buzz bit is a break down the right. He leaves three Millmoor defenders in his trail and reverses the service, sharp cut back to Ilya from the byline.

Ilya Sashka doesn't hit it – he flips it off the inside of his heel somehow, and the ball snaps across the goal, strikes the inside of the post and rebounds into the back of the net.

So Buzz has given Ilya one back, hasn't he?

3–0 to City.

Buzz is fired up.

4–0 before half-time. Ilya has scored again – Buzz had made the space for him, drawing the defence, and Ilya came in from the back and slotted it home.

Just on the half-time whistle, Rotherham get one back.

Nice headed goal, well worked, and it gives their fans something to cheer about.

4–1 to City.

To be fair to the crowd at Millmoor, they know what they're seeing. They haven't been getting at their lads because they're watching one of those special nights by a big player, aren't they?

And they're seeing something *new* as well – a youngster, just at the start of his career – and *different* – young Matt is great on the ball, has the vision, and possibly more speed now than Ilya Sashka had at his best. But that night, though Buzz is getting the goals, Ilya is running the show.

They go 5–1 soon after half-time, and then Ilya goes off.

He waves to the crowd, and they rise to him – the Rotherham supporters as much as City's travelling lot. They know they've seen something they can tell their grandchildren about – a real virtuoso display from a guy in the twilight of his career, who has turned it on in a nothing game.

And I'm thinking, *There goes a legend.*

Ike Stevens comes on. Different type of player.

Like Buzz, he has pace to burn when he wants to. But this night he doesn't seem to want to, or maybe it isn't happening for him. A cold night at Millmoor, the game is won, and he's been put out to stretch his legs.

Stevens doesn't try very hard, does he? He's thinking about Saturday's game with United. He wants out of this without aggravating the injury he's already carrying. They've given him a run in the last quarter of an hour to see if the injury holds up, but he's taking no chances.

The new pairing work two or three neat little interchanges, trying to make plays for each other because Stevens is *good* – in his day one of the best – but it just doesn't work out.

He makes one good chance for Buzz, but

Buzz miskicks when all he had to do was tap it in. Then he makes another, and Buzz over-elaborates and loses the ball. Stevens has his hands on his hips, and he gestures, *You threw that away*.

But Buzz is still up for it. This is his chance, and he's going to take it, is what's in his head. He's still working right to the whistle. He plays the full ninety, flat out.

That's what I really loved in that game. Teddy Maher's Rotherham may not be world-beaters, but they're no slouches. They've been run around by a team way above them in class, but they stick at it and they keep playing football, so Buzz is up against the best opposition he has yet faced.

It's a brilliant night for the boy. Even Teddy Maher gives him a clap on the back, and I'm wondering, *Does Teddy remember that under-14 game years ago at Town, when he first saw the lad?* Maybe he does; maybe he doesn't. You can never tell with Teddy.

When Buzz comes off the field Ilya Sashka is up from the bench, shaking his hand, and everyone in the City camp is happy … except Stevens. He trudges off like he never wants to see Millmoor again.

I'm well pleased with the way Buzz has performed, and Bob's word is that the team at City are delighted. He's given them exactly what they were hoping for.

Saturday, Buzz still doesn't make the bench against United.

He's there in his City jacket with his City tie and his little grey uniform trousers, sitting in the Old Trafford stand.

Ike Stevens gets the winner on a through ball from Ilya Sashka, who has been brought back in because the Manchester United defensive set-up suits his game and because Barbazzi is out with a thigh strain.

"Should have been me!" Buzz tells me afterwards.

And he has a point.

It could have been Buzz – maybe it *should* have been – but it wasn't.

City need every point if they're going to maintain their challenge for the Premiership title, and they're not going to take unneccessary risks with a boy of his age.

What Buzz needs is an injury or two among the front men. Or a few suspensions. Till that happens, he's going to be tapping his heels.

Which is bad news for Buzz.

BAYERN MUNICH v CITY

CHAMPIONS LEAGUE SEMI-FINAL, SECOND LEG
VENUE: OLYMPIC STADIUM, MUNICH

Not many English players can claim that they played in a Champions League semi-final before making their Premiership début. But Buzz did.

In January, City moved two points clear at the top of the Premiership table, but then the injury problems of a hard season started to pile up. A patched-up team struggled through February.

Still no place for Buzz. He's played twice more in the League Cup, scoring two against Bournemouth, but draws a blank in the defeat at Blackburn that put them out of that competition. Buzz is playing regularly for the reserves, and he's improving all the time and getting on the score sheet, but it's mostly empty stadium stuff.

Despite not being in the first team, his name is mentioned in the press, and there is a call-up to the England under-21 squad – against Norway in Oslo. But he doesn't make the team, and Buzz is getting the fidgets again.

"If he doesn't play me, he should put me out on loan somewhere – get me some first-team experience for next year," a despondent Buzz argued.

And I talked to Bob about it again. But Erik wasn't having it.

"Boy has to be patient. Tell him his time will come," Bob told me. "Erik isn't letting him go anywhere. He's working the boy every day, himself. He thinks he's found one."

"We found him!" I tell Bob. "You and me and Alan."

"Don't say that to Erik!" Bob grins back.

So I told Buzz to hang in there and keep trying.

"What's the use?" Buzz said angrily. "I'm not sticking it out here if I never get a game in the first team."

With the injury crisis continuing, Erik has him on the bench for three games, and all of them go down to the wire, but still Buzz doesn't get on.

In March, City's form stutters, with consecutive home draws against Everton and an improving Blackburn, a setback at Bolton and a win at Fulham. The month ended with a defeat at Spurs, leaving City two points adrift of Newcastle and Arsenal, with games in hand over Man U and Liverpool. The Gunners seemed best placed, coming off the unexpected defeat by Malmo, which had ended their European campaign but left them free to concentrate on the Premiership.

City's crushing defeat of Barcelona, home and away, in the Champions League quarter-finals further complicated their fixture list, but it did spark off a revival of form, and they moved to second in the league, behind Liverpool and a point ahead of Arsenal, as the climax of the season approached.

When the home leg of the semi-final against Bayern Munich was played, Buzz wasn't even close to being involved. Ilya Sashka came on late second half, didn't contribute much, and they got turned over by an away goal. 0–1 in Bayern Munich's favour – a goal from a Nurenov free kick from twenty yards out – which wasn't the result City wanted.

Erik had a fourth striker on the bench ... but it wasn't Buzz.

Then, with the away leg of the Champions League semi looming, a fresh clutch of injuries and suspensions got them down to the bare bones of a striking force and Buzz found himself on the plane to Munich with an outside chance of playing.

Erik Goethe made the best he could of it for the press. *The boy is a real talent. If we have to use him ... he's ready.* All that stuff. But the glum faces in the City boot room told their own story.

If their top strikers didn't make it, the choice lay between Willie Jardine and Buzz – which shows you just how great City's squad was. Everybody's dream-team *now* – Buzz and Willie Jardine together – but *then* City's fans were dazed when they read those two names in the sports pages.

The two lads are sitting together on the plane, and they're not nattering much, toying with their airline food – no wonder they didn't eat.

I move down to join Bob Lambetter at the back ... and I'm as bad as Buzz. My stomach is in a knot. I start quizzing him about Buzz's prospects.

"Who am I talking to?" Bob asks me, sharply enough. "My old mate Mickey Griff, or the Mickey Griff who's covering the story for *Intoni Sport International*?"

"I won't print anything you don't want me to," I tell him. "Honest."

"Well then, Buzz isn't just here for the trip. I reckon he's well ahead of the other boy. But it's Erik's choice. It's a toss-up between them who makes the line-up ... but don't tell Buzz that, will you?" Bob says. "Look, I want it as much as you do ... but it isn't my choice. I think that's the way Erik's mind is working, though."

I'm churning inside. What's Buzz feeling if I am as bad as that?

Morning of the semi, and Erik and Bob are still working on it. The news is good and bad. Ilya does ten minutes stretching and warm-up with Bob ... then he raises his arms, thumbs up. He's in. But the other striker is out – as it always seemed he would be. So the question is: who is going to play up front alongside Ilya?

When Erik Goethe reads his team sheet out at the press conference, he confirms that he's starting with Willie Jardine, leaving Buzz on the bench. *And neither Willie nor Buzz*, Erik stresses, *is available for interview till after the game.*

"That goes for you too, *Uncle* Mickey!" he tells me, and all the journos have a laugh at my expense.

My old boss at Town summed it up in the usual Teddy-Maher style on the Sky panel before kick-off.

"Jezz has to be a youngster out of his depth. They'll only use him if they have to. You know what I'd do? I'd play in an extra defender instead. Go with young Jardine and Ilya

Sashka up front alone, and hang in there. My way, they might pinch one on the break, hold out for penalties. Realistically, penalties are City's best chance. This way – playing two up in a game like this and going for the away goal they need – is just asking for trouble. You can't come to Munich and try all-out attack when you have your choice strikers on the treatment table or out suspended, can you? I'm hoping for a result for City, but we could be looking at Bayern Munich going through by two or three goals, without conceding – if it all goes to form, that is. Young Jezz would be clear out of his depth in a game of this importance, if you ask me. He's an irrelevance."

Luckily, Erik Goethe hadn't asked Teddy, but nobody on the panel pointed that out. Possibly because Teddy had taken a walk from the job at Millmoor and wound up advising Gravesend and Northfleet, and Erik was just a handful of games away from winning City's first ever Premiership title.

That was it. The teams were warming up.

Going into the game, the general verdict was that Bayern would play cautiously, letting City come at them, and kill a depleted City on the break. They had the vital away goal going for them – they didn't have to push it. They could afford to hold on, and let City make the effort.

"German mentality," is Teddy's witless verdict. "This could be like a visit to the dentist for City – all pain and no toffee. City haven't the guns or the ammo to go blazing at them, and Bayern will kill the game with efficiency and settle for what they've got."

This is Nurenov's Bayern Munich. They haven't been listening to Teddy. They're up for it.

The first ten minutes are Bayern, Bayern, Bayern and Bayern again – beautiful stuff, all guns blazing. They are out to get two or three goals and kill a weakened City team. Nurenov is everywhere. Erik has told his defenders to man-mark him out of it, and they're doing all they can, but how do you mark someone like that with two good feet and will-o'-the-wisp talent?

On or off the ball, Nurenov is a danger, not to mention free kicks anywhere near the box.

But this is City, isn't it? Niall Dunne, Marceno, Skeate, Barbazzi … they haven't come to be bossed about. Dunne gets on top of their wideman, and starts making his own runs forward. Marceno is on his game, probing, passing, playing those deadly flighted balls into the area for old Ilya. Skeate is on top of his game, showing why he has to be the best midfielder in England … barring Bower, that is.

148

City have survived the first ten minutes of Bayern pressure, and now the game's beginning to swing around. City are on top. Bayern are restricted to the corners and dead balls, and even then they aren't showing much.

"City are hammering them now ... but have nothing to show for it!" Teddy tells the Sky world out there.

Ilya Sashka has no pace and is nursing an injury, and Bayern know it... But he's a clever old fox. He doesn't hide himself. He's taking the game to them, even with his restricted movement. And young Willie Jardine is a miracle. He's up front with Ilya. They're working together, with Barbazzi coming from behind ... and they throw out some really good stuff. Willie has little snake hips, and a way of drawing defenders onto him and then releasing the ball into space for Marceno coming from the back.

Marceno puts Barbazzi clean through on goal... Keeper saves it.

Then Ilya has a blaster himself – loose ball he moved onto outside the area. No time to think ... but he hits a rocket that cannons off the inside of the post and back into the keeper's arms.

City must have made eight or nine clear-cut chances, coming up to half-time ... but the ball won't go in. After a slow start, they have run Bayern ragged, played them out of the game ... but they need that away goal, and it won't come.

Half-time. And City are still 0–0, with the away goal from the first leg against them.

Ilya Sashka limps off. He has Erik Goethe talking in his ear and gesturing, and the physio is trotting alongside him.

"You know what?" Teddy Maher tells the Sky audience. "That old warhorse has done all he can, I reckon. The way he's moving now, he won't make it second half."

For once, Teddy is right.

Ilya didn't make it out for the second half.

Buzz did.

City line up for the second half with Barbazzi and Buzz up front, and Willie Jardine out wide. This leaves them short in midfield, which is not the City way and is an odd formation, but Erik had to do something because they're losing on the away goal. I'm just hoping Buzz can hold his own out there, now his chance has come.

Fifty-second minute Barbazzi goes up with the keeper, who flails at the ball. It could have gone anywhere. Where it goes is straight to Buzz, unmarked on the penalty spot.

Buzz volleys it in towards goal.

The keeper parries it ... there's a melee in front of the goal ... defender tries to clear ... prods it into his own net.

The Bayern players pick the ball out of the

net. They're gesturing at each other, passing the blame. But City are back in the tie.

Erik Goethe and Bob are up off the bench. I'm up dancing and roaring my head off in the press box.

City are 0–1 up, which means the teams are tied at 1–1 on aggregate.

Teddy goes bananas. "Kill 'em off now, City will!" he tells his viewers.

Buzz and young Jardine both have pace – and not just ordinary pace. Erik has told them to use it, and they do. And Buzz isn't the only star out there. Barbazzi is mixing it, and young Jardine is dancing and flicking and laying balls off and tearing them apart with his speed and it looks as if City's Champions League campaign is right back on course.

Barbazzi slices one wide, after Buzz and Jardine have played a neat little interchange and put him clear.

Marceno puts Niall Dunne clear. Dunne swings it over. Buzz comes roaring in out of nowhere – he's found space again – takes the ball first time and smacks it against the left upright. It comes back out ... Buzz lunges for it ... the defender lunges too. Lifts Buzz, not the ball. Buzz is flat out in the area ... penalty!

Ref waves play on.

Bayern go down the other end, hopeful ball into the box, the keeper comes to gather, fumbles. Niall Dunne nips in and clears off the line.

Buzz again. Barbazzi plays him through. Buzz goes to play it back to him, seems to hesitate, then the kid is past his man and heading in on goal and I'm up off my seat screaming and the defender grabs his shirt and Buzz is down, second time, edge of the box … or just inside.

No penalty. Yellow card for diving.

"Went down too easy!" Teddy Maher tells his audience. "I reckon the kid is tiring already. Not up to this pace."

Then Willie Jardine takes a kick in the face in a tussle down the right-hand corner of the park. Willie needs treatment, and when he gets back on, you can see he's lost it. Bayern's left-back is all smiles and apologies. But he's shaken Willie up, hasn't he? Seen the problem; dealt with it.

With his face swollen and bruised, Willie starts to drift out of the game, despite all the encouragement he's getting from the line.

"Run out of puff, hasn't he – like young Jezz?" Teddy tells his audience gloomily. "City can't afford to put kids out there to do a man's job. Obvious, innit? But they've got to go for it, City, haven't they? Got to find something from somewhere… One spot of inspiration… One … I don't know … bit of magic like they've showed us all season in the

Premiership. But their magicians are all in the treatment room, aren't they?"

Nurenov for Bayern has all the space in the world now, and he starts to use it. Erik Goethe has a face like thunder. Bayern are stringing the passes together, controlling it, forcing City back.

I know what I'd do with this if this was a comic book story.

Barbazzi gets drawn deeper. Young hero Jezz is left up there all alone. He gets the ball on the halfway line. Feints this way, feints that, then he's off. Runs the length of the field, scores, saves the game for City. Then he does it again. And again. Hat-trick! Takes the ball home as a gift for his lovely girlfriend, the model.

It doesn't happen like that. This is for real, not a story.

This is a European Champions League semi; Bayern Munich are Bayern Munich. They have been knocked back by City's goal, but they don't panic. What they have to do is keep playing their game and wait for something to happen that will finish City off.

City keep coming, pressing and pressing and pressing. Barbazzi is playing out of his skin. But it isn't happening for them.

Jardine is still on the groggy side, but he's signalling to the bench that he wants to stay on – isn't doing much though, understandably.

153

Buzz is drawn further and further back, hunting the ball. There's no way City are going to get back into it, but, despite Teddy's comment, young Matt's still running, harrying, working ... and looking for the breaks up front.

Bayern know the clock is ticking.

They've run out of ideas up front, but they start passing it about.

"Tragedy for City if this goes wrong!" Teddy is telling the Sky viewers.

The message Bayern Munich are sending to to City is: *Come and win the ball. Then, when you try that, we've got the pace and guile to break down your end and finish the game.*

That's what's in Nurenov's head anyway ... and he's running the game from the Munich point of view.

He's stopped going forward. He's going sideways.

And then ... sloppy ball.

Bayern's best player on the night, Nurenov, and he's laying it off, and he miscues.

And suddenly, almost unbelievably, a limping and exhausted Barbazzi has the ball at his feet, and no one between him and the goal.

They're haring back after him, defenders closing in from either side. He's still thirty yards out, there's no support, and he knows he hasn't the legs to carry on his run, and really there's nothing he can do but lash it.

The Bayern keeper is off his line.

The ball arcs off Barbazzi's foot, over the keeper, who is at full stretch, bending back, clawing for it. Going over the bar, looks like, from where I'm sitting.

But it hits the underside of the bar, bounces down, hits the keeper as he falls, and he grabs despairingly, but all he's grabbing is air, as the ball bounces away off him...

Goes for a corner, which comes to nothing. Full-time.

0–1 to City on the night, still 1–1 on aggregate.

"Perfect skill!" Teddy Maher purrs, when he's got his breath back. "Some footballer, that!"

The perfect skill is in Teddy's dream.

It was hit-and-hope time. Even Barbazzi admits it later.

The game is heading for extra time.

"Best we could have hoped for," Teddy purrs. "Now it comes down to which team wants it most, doesn't it?"

That year, the golden goal had been dropped. We're back with fifteen minutes each way.

"Maybe they can still do it despite all their injuries," Teddy tells the viewers. "I reckon Bayern are knackered. It's a circus, this... Bring on the clowns!"

He's on his wishful high again, isn't he?

155

Tells the viewers that Bayern have let it slip. City have the initiative. They will go at Bayern, all or nothing, tear them apart. Complete contradiction of everything he has said up to now – a complete nonsense, but it sounds patriotic and goes down well with the panel.

The truth is, you don't tear a team like Bayern apart. Not with Nurenov and his mates out there. And they don't tear a team like City apart either.

They're both good teams. It's a toss-up between them going into extra time.

Bayern's heads are down a bit with losing the advantage of the away goal, but they're playing some beautiful controlled stuff, pulling a tiring City back line all over the shop. When they have the ball, that is.

When City have it, Barbazzi is making his runs and Buzz is playing like he's been a star turn all year. Twists, turns ... makes space.

Willie Jardine has a header that comes down off the bar, bounces on the line, and gets cleared off Dunne's foot just as he's going to turn it in.

At the other end, City's keeper turns one over the bar that he has no right to reach.

Bayern are chasing now, in their own fashion, but making City work, and work again. The team chasing the ball is the team that runs out of steam first.

Buzz is still showing up everywhere. He gets one-on-one, touches the ball past the last defender, then loses out to the kind of rash tackle that should have the defender booked ... but doesn't.

"That's three penalties the kid could have had!" Teddy tells us.

The teams change round; still 1–1 on aggregate.

Second half, Bayern stop going forward.

City aren't doing much either.

"It's down to who makes a mistake now!" Teddy drones on.

Nobody does.

Funny how a game can die like that in extra time.

The game trails to an end – Bayern are out of ideas, and City have nothing left but the occasional bit of ball play from Buzz, and Dunne's attempt from a free kick that goes nearer the corner flag than the goal.

So it's 1–1 on aggregate, and City have cancelled the away goal advantage ... in a game that could have yielded three or four goals, either side.

I'm thinking, *From Matt's point of view, it's the game that makes him, because Erik Goethe has pitched him in and the boy has more than held his own, hasn't he? A manager like Erik would have to be well pleased with a kid performing so well in a game at this level.*

157

"Youngster did well. Could have earned a penalty ... gets carded instead. But there, wouldn't hold that against him. Kid has earned his corn, hasn't he? More than! By the end, like everybody else, he's run out of puff and ideas. Thought it might go that way!" is Teddy's self-serving summary of Buzz's day, up to that point.

It is down to penalties. Bayern win the toss, decide to go first.

Bayern score the first one.

City miss.

It is 1–0 Bayern. Four to go.

City's keeper saves with his feet ... and City score.

So we're 1–1 with two kicks taken and three each to go.

Bayern score. 2–1.

Barbazzi gets his second goal of the game to equalize.

2–2, with two penalties out of the five remaining.

The giant Barbazzi waves to the City fans and they cheer him like he's just won the thing.

Only, City haven't won it ... not yet. They haven't even won the semi-final.

Bayern miss their next kick ... so do City.

Each team has one penalty left. Still tied at 2–2.

Bayern have been saving Nurenov for the last crucial kick.

He picks his spot, and City's keeper can't reach it.

So Bayern are winning it 3–2.

City's turn – equalize, or they're out. No Champions League this year. Score, and we go to sudden death.

Niall Dunne takes it. The keeper goes the right way, gets a hand on it … pushes it onto the inside of the post, but it cannons into the net.

3–3.

The five penalties are up, the scores are still tied, and now it is sudden death.

The Bayern guy trots up, puts the ball on the spot, crosses himself … and misses by a mile. Balloons it over the bar.

He goes down on his knees, clutching his head. And there's nobody in the game who wouldn't weep for him. It was his big moment; now it's something he'll never be allowed to forget. He's just handed the semi to City, hasn't he? All they have to do is score, and City are in the final.

The next man up for City is … *Matt*.

A kid like Buzz shouldn't have *this* number on his plate. There are old City pros out there who have edged out and refused to take it on when Erik Goethe was going round with his *Are-you-up-for-it? Do-you-want-to-take-one?* question.

I'm praying he won't miss it – because if he

does, he'll never live it down, will he? *The kid who threw away City's chance...*

It's typical of Buzz that he doesn't chicken out or hold back.

He just puts the ball on the spot carefully, and takes a few paces back.

Even if he misses, I tell myself, *Buzz has come of age.*

And you know what? He *doesn't* miss.

Calm as you like, he sends the keeper one way, rolls the ball the other.

Slots it. Not one of his screamers, but precise, and unstoppable. Just the winning goal ... that's all.

4–3. And City are in the Champions League final for the first time ever.

There's no handspring from Buzz this time. He's pale, Buzz is. City are mobbing him and high-handing him and Erik Goethe and Bob Lambetter are dancing over the pitch.

Me?

I'm sitting there with a grin from ear to ear.

'Cause my boy done it, didn't he?

He took the penalty on ... and *slotted* it.

Eat your heart out, Teddy Maher... My little lad did it, all by his own little self.

LIVERPOOL v CITY

PREMIERSHIP

VENUE: ANFIELD

Liverpool versus City at Anfield. It was the day Buzz wrote his name in the history books.

Liverpool away is a tough fixture at any time, and City were still carrying injuries to key players as they came into the last game of their Premiership season – a game City had to win to pip Arsenal for the title ... with the possibility of a Champions League–Premiership double still there, if they could beat Real Madrid in the final. City were level on points with the Gunners, who were playing a struggling Everton at Highbury, but Arsenal had the better goal difference by far and were odds-on favourites for the title.

The game was crucial for Liverpool as well.

They were still in with a shout of a Champions League place ... if other results went in their favour at St James' Park and Stamford Bridge.

Buzz had made a huge impression on manager Erik Goethe in Munich and in two appearances as sub in the Premiership games that followed ... but he still wouldn't have made the line-up for this crucial match if others had been available. They weren't.

Ilya Sashka and Bobov both failed fitness tests. Stevens was suspended. So it came down to the question of a starting partner for Barbazzi, who was filling in for them up front, playing out of position – though the big man will always do a good job anywhere, as Italy found out in the World Cup Finals.

The only alternative to playing Barbazzi up front, was to go with Buzz and Willie Jardine, but, even for Erik Goethe, that was too big a risk.

It came down to a choice between the two lads ... and this time Erik went for Buzz, largely on the strength of his performance in Munich.

It meant a patched-up City team going into the game on which the success or failure of their whole season depended.

Teddy Maher was his usual sweet self in his match preview for Sky. "You wouldn't want to play the Buzz-boy, would you? Good in parts as he was in Munich. It is too much to load on a young and inexperienced prospect like Jezz; even if he is the player Erik makes him out to be. Liverpool will be up for it – they have the extra Champions League spot to play for. They will lean on the lad early on – you can count on that. For my money I'd have started with young Jardine out wide. He'd have given them extra options ... but there you go. Maybe Erik can bring the lad Jardine on second half... But by then it could be too late."

As usual, Teddy's forecasting proved to be wrong, explosively wrong.

I was there on another of my one-off broadcasting contracts for the Prossi Organization, who were relaying it to Scandinavia – good money too.

So I'm with Gunnar Largsen, the ex Swedish international, who is on a permanent contract with Prossi. He is handling the Scandinavian commentary; I'm the back-up man feeding him notes, and we're watching the teams come out.

"You know what?" I tell Gunnar. "I've a hunch this is young Buzz's big day."

Gunnar smiles, shrugs and goes back to his notes.

"It's set up for him," I go on. "When I had the kid at Hollins and Parborough he—"

"Mickey," Gunnar says, "you tell me this romance already three times today, twice on the flight, OK? Save it for the boys in the bar later ... *if* young Buzz pulls it off for you in the game."

Then we are into the game.

Liverpool are up for it ... very. And when you see the team they have out – Craigie, Dunwoody, Wilkenson, Macken, Del Hondre leading the attack – you've got to wonder if a depleted City can hold them.

The breaking news is that Erik has done something that no one expected. The giant Barbazzi, who was supposed to be leading the line, is playing off Buzz ... not the other way about.

"What is this that Erik does?" Gunnar asks me.

Nothing too complicated, I'm thinking.

"Pace," I tell him. And that is what it is.

Buzz is right there up front, going wide either side, pulling them apart – with the midfielders cutting through into the holes he has made, and Barbazzi knocking lumps out of Craigie and Dunwoody.

Erik has strung four City shirts across the park, five when Barbazzi pulls back, but this is not defensive. They are bombing forward, taking the game to Liverpool, trying to knock the home team out of their stride. And the yellow and black City shirts are everywhere.

Then Craigie breaks out from the back, plays Del Hondre through, and the big Dutchman goes down in the box under Skeate's challenge.

Penalty kick.

Craigie comes up from the back, and takes it. Slots it home. 1–0 to Liverpool. The Scousers are chanting, singing, rejoicing as Barbazzi kicks off.

Buzz is on the ball, plays it square, goes past his man, gets it back, dinks it to the far post and Skeate, up like a bird, nods it back for Barbazzi, who prods it home.

1–1. And only a quarter of an hour gone. This time, the City fans are the ones who are roaring.

It is getting tough out there. The tackles are flying. No one is hanging back ... particularly in City's half of the field, where Del Hondre seems intent on taking on the entire City back four by himself. He's in there, flailing around, causing disruption.

City aren't coping as well as they might ... but they get away with it.

A screamer from Macken is beaten down by the City keeper and Del Hondre dives in, gets his header on goal, and the keeper tips it up in the air.

Skeate clears it off the line.

Down the other end, Buzz takes a ball on

his chest, leans in, turns Dunwoody, leaving the big guy flat-footed. Craigie comes in, up-ends him, and Craigie gets a yellow card – which he has been asking for from the whistle.

Buzz gets up, walks towards the ball, nods to the ref, plays it while they are still getting sorted. Barbazzi is through on goal, draws the keeper; Buzz is square – Barbazzi plays the ball to him.

Buzz taps it into the net.

Liverpool go mad. They are crowding round the ref and arguing with him. Dunwoody gets a yellow when he carries it too far. So now they have two men yellow-carded already, and Del Hondre up front treading a very narrow line.

The ref sticks with it...

2–1 in City's favour.

Liverpool have lost an early lead; now they're a goal behind, and they see all the efforts of their season, including the eighteen points from six games in November/December, drifting away from them.

They really go at City.

Everyone is back – Buzz, Barbazzi even – they're slotting out wide when the reds have the ball, covering the flanks. And for the ten minutes after the goal it is one-way traffic.

Del Hondre gets clear ... misses.

Macken has a penalty appeal turned down

... more mouthing at the ref.

Then Macken loses out on another one. High ball in, edge of the area; he's trying to get across the defender; he goes down. Gets up, yelling that his shirt was pulled.

Yellow for Niall Dunne.

"That was a penalty, Mickey," Gunnar tells me. "Had to be." But the ref rules it outside.

Liverpool are still piling it on.

Del Hondre is clean through on goal, scuffs his shot. The keeper beats it out, and the follow-up clips the post, and it goes for a goal kick.

Forty-two minutes gone ... and City are on the attack for once. Buzz has the ball, out wide left. Barbazzi is making ground in the middle. Buzz goes to play him in, then jinks inside himself. What was he...? Twenty ... thirty yards out, closing in on the edge of the box. Liverpool are backing off, trying to pick up the midfielders coming through.

Mistake. Never back off. Tend to first things first ... close him down ... particularly if it's Buzz.

Hits a screamer. Edge of the box, curling in low to the bottom corner. The keeper gets a glove on it, but the shot is so hot that he can't turn it around for a corner. The ball bangs the foot of the post, and winds up in the net.

The Buzz thing again. No back-lift. No

167

nothing. One minute, he's in full stride, bearing down on goal, considering the options, looks like he'll cut it back. The next, the ball is nestling in the back of the net.

3–1 to City.

Buzz is doing cartwheels. The City guys are all over him. The fans are going mad behind the away goal.

That's the way they go in at half-time.

"Mickey," Gunnar says, turning to me, "maybe you better tell me your story again!"

The news from Highbury is that Arsenal are also winning – 1–0 – but according to the commentary they are stuttering. Everton have been making a game of it. So it isn't all done and dusted.

If City can keep Liverpool out in the second half they might just do it.

Molde for Dunne at the back is the only City change at half-time – Niall has a back strain, officially, but probably Erik has the yellow card in his mind. Doesn't want to be down to ten men – which he could be if Niall gets a tackle wrong.

Liverpool are sticking with the side they started with.

The second half gets underway with the reds probing, playing the ball about. They are hard and well organized, and they have forty-five minutes to put it right … if they

can. With the right results at St James'
Park, where Newcastle have Blackburn, and
Stamford Bridge, where Chelsea are already
one down, Liverpool might just squeak
through to a Champions League place even if
they lose this one – but they can't chance it,
can they?

They've got to go for it.

Not in the first ten minutes, they don't.
That's controlled, almost quiet, after the
mayhem that followed Buzz's goal for City
just before half-time.

Craigie has cooled down. He's in there
bossing things in midfield, and this is probably Liverpool's best spell in the game.
They're not throwing everything forward,
just playing, passing, working the angles and
the channels brilliantly, and hoping for a
break.

No break comes.

Erik's defence has been brilliant all season,
and they have a two goal cushion, so they
are taking no risks. It's like a chess game out
there, till Del Hondre gets onto a beautifully
flighted ball from Dunwoody that takes his
marker out.

He slots it. 65 minutes 30 seconds.

2–3 to City now … but Liverpool, believing
they can do it again, are sweeping forward, but
the clock is beginning to tick against them …
and they're taking risks.

Erik Goethe is up from the bench, talking, calling, and Dino Zan for Liverpool is at the same game. Head up, arms flailing, shouting, urging ... because he can see what's happening.

They're pressing and pressing and pressing, but it's getting too quick, too frantic. They need someone to put a foot on the ball.

So they change it, and Walter Lukie comes on for Liverpool.

He's deceptive, Lukie. Doesn't look like he's doing much, but he can change a game. Grab it by the throat.

Suddenly he's controlling midfield, spraying the ball around. City try to reorganize, cut out the supply to him, but he just pops up somewhere else. He's all over the place, full of running, playing for this one – their Champions League spot – and his Euro place with France as well ... 'cause he's slipped down the rankings with France since joining Liverpool, and he needs a big performance.

Big game player – Walter Lukie – everyone knows that.

Now he's showing how he won that reputation.

Some of the stuff he's pulling off is magic. He's strutting, in control, tearing the City rearguard apart with his sheer technical skill on the ball, and his vision.

Walter's on the ball for Liverpool, in his own half.

Pinpoint pass to Craigie. Gets it back. Reverse pass to the midfield. Gets it back. Long ball to Craigie, who has moved on fast, finding the opening. Craigie takes it on the chest, slips his man, lays it back across the face of the area.

Lukie again ... moving onto it. Picks his spot. Hits it.

Keeper saves ... fumbles ... drops it, the ball breaks clear. Del Hondre has the goal at his mercy. Barbazzi takes it off his toe and clears the ball for City.

What's the big man doing there? How has he got back? Doesn't matter ... he has. Measure of the pressure City have been under.

Now City have the ball. They're breaking up field.

Buzz is wide for City, all on his own. Takes on Dunwoody. Dunwoody half drags him to the ground by the back of the shirt – only way the Liverpool player could stop him – ref waves it on while Buzz is moaning.

Dunwoody plays the ball up field – wild, loose clearance.

Lukie comes across the defender, nods it on.

Del Hondre picks it up for Liverpool, edge of the area, shuffles, changes stride, clips it.

The ball was heading high and wide, but Skeate is roaring in for City, near post and the keeper has gone missing, so he's scared to let it go in case someone is there behind him.

Takes on the header, trying to turn it for a corner.

Own goal – unstoppable.

3–3. Seventy-eighth minute. Liverpool are back in it.

We've hardly restarted when the crowd erupts down the City end.

Equalizer at Highbury. Everton are holding the Gunners 1–1, all against the run of play. But it doesn't matter, does it? 1–1 at Highbury, 3–3 at Anfield, and City are going to miss out on the title.

So the game has changed again.

Now City have to chase it.

Marceno comes off; Willie Jardine is on.

Buzz to Willie, Willie to Buzz ... Barbazzi gets a nod on.

Willie is through on goal, squares it across. Buzz has come off his marker, gets on the end of it. Liverpool keeper saves it. Ball comes out. Skeate blasts it over the top.

That's the eighty-third minute, according to the clock.

Chelsea are two behind at the Bridge; Newcastle and Blackburn are scoreless ... so the results are right for Liverpool. All they have to do is hold it at 3–3, and the draw will give them their Champions League spot.

And now it's all *Willie–Willie–Willie.*

The little kid is doing what he does now for Scotland – all his own way.

Buzz and Barbazzi are rampaging up the middle. Skeate and Crossan and Declare have forgotten all about defending for City – defeat doesn't matter, because of the way the game at Highbury is going.

A draw is no use to City.

They have to win it.

And Willie Jardine is chopped down by Craigie, edge of the box. By rights it should have been another yellow – but he's been yellow-carded already and two yellows would have him off.

The ref calls Craigie to him, tongue wagging … but he stays on. Feels like a home-town decision to me.

They line up the free kick.

Jardine was brought down wide left, but there is an angle if Skeate goes for it.

Liverpool are lined up, pushing, shoving and making themselves obnoxious.

Skeate blasts it against the wall.

Has to be taken again, encroaching.

Eighty-nine minutes gone … and counting.

Willie Jardine runs up to take it for City … and steps over the ball.

Skeate, coming from behind him, drifts a great ball in, far post.

Del Hondre rises for it – six-foot-four striker, back defending in his own box.

Keeper leaves it to him. No bother.

And suddenly …

Buzz is across them both, coming from Del Hondre's blind side.

Rises like a bird. No chance with the big striker, if Del Hondre knows he's coming. But the big man doesn't spot it till it's too late … and Buzz is across him, nodding the ball down just inside the post.

Hat-trick for Buzz.

3–4 to City.

He's off – somersaults, arms in the air, tears his shirt off. The whole City bench are up on the pitch, yelling and screaming, and the City fans are chanting and singing, and the place is in an uproar.

Meanwhile, the ref is after Buzz.

Yellow card for excessive celebration – some mothers do have 'em!

Buzz pulls his shirt back on, gets back to the centre, slowly.

And that's it.

Three minutes injury time, and Willie Jardine plays most of it out in a duet with the corner flag at the Liverpool end.

Whistle goes.

Then they're on the pitch, waiting.

And the Highbury result comes through.

1–1. Everton have held on.

And it is …

CITY–CITY–CITY, from their end.

For me, in the box, it is …
BUZZ–BUZZ–BUZZ!
My little lad.
And he's done it.

Hat-trick in the last game of the season … and City have the title, with the Champions League final against Real Madrid still to come.

"Mickey," Gunnar says to me in the commentary box. "Mickey … that's valuable company equipment you're dancing on, Mickey."

"Yes!" I'm yelling. "Yes–Yes–Yes!"

"Mickey…"

"BUZZ–BUZZ–BUZZ!" I'm chanting with the fans.

And that's it.

The rest of Buzz's story has been told many times… I don't have to fill it in for you, do I?

It was the first of City's three consecutive Premiership titles, and they got compensation for losing the game against Real Madrid by coming back to dominate the Champions League the following year, when Buzz and Willie Jardine took Inter apart in the final.

Buzz… What more can I say about Buzz, that you don't already know from the tabloids? Nothing – he's up there where he belongs now: in the England squad, with the world knocking at his door.

175

It is all a long way from the day at Scrubs when I went dog-walking; the dimly lit kick-about match at the back of the Boro stand; the Sam King stand-off against Kingstonian; the third round Cup tie when we lost out to Millwall in the closing minutes; the Big Macs in my car after Declan Brody did his bit of smart business over Steve; the night when Ilya Sashka and Buzz set Millmoor alight.

Me, I'm still living it.

You know what I like best about it ... me, Mickey Griff?

I found the new shooting star, I did!